"I don't like the idea of your going in alone. It's too risky."

"There's no other way," Bolan replied. "Only one man at a time can take the ladder. A second man would have to wait for me to get up and into the bunker anyway. Once that happens the war is over. They get me or I get them. There's not going to be any middle ground."

The warrior didn't wait for an argument. He aimed the light down the tunnel and moved on. The next ladder was nearly a hundred fifty yards away.

The Executioner began to climb, then pressed an ear against the hatch. He could hear talking on the other side. "That's the last of them," a voice said. "I'll be back in half an hour. I have some unfinished business, then I want to take care of the Chirkizian woman."

Bolan climbed back down and checked his watch. "He's just leaving. You've got three minutes, Don."

Marshack was already up and running, his light bobbing up and down along the lichen-covered bricks. The warrior checked the hands of his watch once more, then headed back up the ladder.

The Executioner was alone in the dark. And it was time.

MACK BOLAN®

The Executioner

#135 Devil Force	Stony Man Doctrine
#136 Down and Dirty	Terminal Velocity
#137 Battle Lines	Resurrection Day
#138 Kill Trap	Dirty War
#139 Cutting Edge	Flight 741
#140 Wild Card	Dead Easy
#141 Direct Hit	Sudden Death
#142 Fatal Error	Rogue Force
#143 Helldust Cruise	Tropic Heat
#144 Whipsaw	Fire in the Sky
#145 Chicago Payoff	Anvil of Hell
#146 Deadly Tactics	Flash Point
#147 Payback Game	Flesh and Blood
#148 Deep and Swift	Moving Target
#149 Blood Rules	Tightrope
#150 Death Load	Blowout
#151 Message to Medellín	Blood Fever
#152 Combat Stretch	Knockdown
#153 Firebase Florida	Assault
#154 Night Hit	Backlash
#155 Hawaiian Heat	Siege
#156 Phantom Force	Blockade
#157 Cayman Strike	Evil Kingdom
#158 Firing Line	Counterblow
#159 Steel and Flame	Hardline
#160 Storm Warning	Firepower
#161 Eye of the Storm	Storm Burst
#162 Colors of Hell	Intercept
#163 Warrior's Edge	Lethal Impact
#164 Death Trail	Deadfall
#165 Fire Sweep	
#166 Assassin's Creed	
#167 Double Action	
#168 Blood Price	
#169 White Heat	
#170 Baja Blitz	
#171 Deadly Force	

DON PENDLETON'S
THE EXECUTIONER®
FEATURING MACK BOLAN®

DEADLY FORCE

A GOLD EAGLE BOOK FROM
WORLDWIDE®

TORONTO • NEW YORK • LONDON
AMSTERDAM • PARIS • SYDNEY • HAMBURG
STOCKHOLM • ATHENS • TOKYO • MILAN
MADRID • WARSAW • BUDAPEST • AUCKLAND

First edition March 1993

ISBN 0-373-61171-4

Special thanks and acknowledgment to
Charlie McDade for his contribution to this work.

DEADLY FORCE

Evil is easy, and has infinite forms.

—Blaise Pascal
1623–1662

Evil to him who evil thinks.

—Edward III
1312–1377

A man must make a stand against the forces of
evil, protect hearth and home against those who
would crush the dream. Or there will be no hope
for tomorrow.

—Mack Bolan

THE
MACK BOLAN®
LEGEND

Nothing less than a war could have fashioned the destiny of the man called Mack Bolan. Bolan earned the Executioner title in the jungle hell of Vietnam.

But this soldier also wore another name—Sergeant Mercy. He was so tagged because of the compassion he showed to wounded comrades-in-arms and Vietnamese civilians.

Mack Bolan's second tour of duty ended prematurely when he was given emergency leave to return home and bury his family, victims of the Mob. Then he declared a one-man war against the Mafia.

He confronted the Families head-on from coast to coast, and soon a hope of victory began to appear. But Bolan had broken society's every rule. That same society started gunning for this elusive warrior—to no avail.

So Bolan was offered amnesty to work within the system against terrorism. This time, as an employee of Uncle Sam, Bolan became Colonel John Phoenix. With a command center at Stony Man Farm in Virginia, he and his new allies—Able Team and Phoenix Force—waged relentless war on a new adversary: the KGB.

But when his one true love, April Rose, died at the hands of the Soviet terror machine, Bolan severed all ties with Establishment authority.

Now, after a lengthy lone-wolf struggle and much soul-searching, the Executioner has agreed to enter an ''arm's-length'' alliance with his government once more, reserving the right to pursue personal missions in his Everlasting War.

PROLOGUE

The Cadillac slowed as it approached the wrought-iron gate, then coasted to a stop. The driver could see the security guards behind the gate, but he looked off into the trees on either side before rolling down his window. Beech trees nearly obscured the high stone wall a dozen feet away. Clumps of flowering shrubs, their thick rubbery leaves glistening with the recent rain, quivered in the breeze, drops of water catching the floodlights and winking like fireflies.

The driver could hear the hum of the powerful electric motor as the gate slid off to one side, disappearing behind the stone wall. One of the guards waved a hand. The driver gunned the engine and drove through the gate, only to be confronted with another. The vehicle was in a box made of iron bars. The sally port wasn't much larger than the car, leaving little room between the rear bumper and the closing gate.

The guard shone a light through the open window. "Sir, may I see your invitation, please?"

The driver grunted, reached up over the sun visor, grabbed the invitation and handed over the thick envelope. A second guard materialized at the first man's shoulder. The driver noticed the name tags, little black plastic rectangles with names etched through to the white underneath. The nearer guard was named Jacques, and his companion was named René, or so the tags read. Neither one looked familiar, and he'd been here dozens of times. He thought about saying something, but what was the point? Guards were like chauffeurs. They came and went at the whim of their employers.

"Mr. and Mrs. Charlton are with you?"

The driver cocked a thumb over his shoulder. The light flicked away from the driver's compartment and filled the rear of the limo with its harsh glare.

"Norman, what's going on? What's all this about?"

Norman Charlton patted his wife on the knee. "Don't pay any attention to this nonsense, Lois. You know what Walter is like. He's just being overcautious. He probably heard something on the news and got uptight again. Every few months he goes through one of these phases. If I had his money, I guess I'd be cautious, too."

The interior gate was already rolling open. The Cadillac lurched ahead, and the sound of tires on gravel filled the car as Charlton pressed the button to raise the window. It was nearly a quarter mile to the house, and the landscaped lawns were studded with lights, most of them concealed in clumps of shrubbery or along the base of the sculpted hedges that wound mazelike across the estate.

The house was huge and brightly lighted. A circular driveway of crushed white marble swept in a broad arc between the two wings of the structure, approaching it most closely in front of the main entrance. A fountain, illuminated by half a dozen floods under the pond, sent glittering cascades over a trio of statues that Walter Jason, their host for the evening, once claimed were originals from a Greek temple.

No one knew whether to believe Jason, because his gift for fantasy was almost the equal of his gift for making money, an art of which he was past master. Both had served him well, however, and no one was sure whether his money or his lying had gotten him the French ambassadorship.

As the car rolled to a stop in front of the wide stairway, Charlton got out of the car and helped his wife out of the vehicle, narrowly beating a liveried attendant to the punch.

Walter Jason himself stood in front of the huge glass doors. When he recognized Charlton, he waved and started down the steps, all smiles when he reached the driveway and stuck out one manicured hand in greeting.

"Glad you could make it, Norm. Lois, you look stunning." He parodied a gallantry he never quite understood and swept the ground with his fingertips, then gave Lois a bear hug more appropriate to the thinly disguised Texan he was. "God almighty, you are a looker," he said, setting her back on the gravel.

"Sorry we're late, Walt," Charlton said.

"Hell, everybody's late these days. That's the way it is, just one more sign that civilization is coming to an end sooner than any of us hoped. Hell, I wanted to spend all my money before Armageddon. Looks like I'll have to rush to do it. Of course, Edith'll help me." He laughed and patted Lois on the shoulder. "You got to build a fire under that man of yours, Lois, so you can help him spend it."

Lois Charlton, who considered Jason something just short of a boor, said, "Walter, God couldn't spend all your money. And Norman is doing just fine, thank you very much."

"Now, now, Lois, don't be spiteful."

Anxious to change the subject, Charlton asked, "Is Steven here yet?"

"Course he is, Norman. Never knew him to turn down a free meal, did you?"

"Never met the man in my life, Walt."

"You will, Norman, you will. Keep your pants on."

Charlton shrugged. He wanted to get down to brass tacks before Lois ran out of patience. He was on the verge of the biggest deal of his life, and both Jason and Aldretti were a big part of it. Jason's electronics firm was plugged into the Pentagon in half a dozen ways, and Steven Aldretti was an undersecretary of the Army, which put him squarely in Jason's pocket. If this deal went through, Charlton was set for life, and he knew it.

They climbed the stairs to the huge French doors that towered fifteen feet above their heads. Lois Charlton looked around her with amazement. Impressive as all hell, she thought, even if Walter was hard to take.

"They're all in the game room, I think," Jason said. "That Rosalie is one beautiful gal. And smart as a whip. No wonder Stevie's doing so well. I thought leaving the Army was a mistake, but I reckon he's better off now than he ever was. Course, you meet a lot of useful folks, make all kind of connections at NATO."

They were descending the stairs to the game room, when a series of short, sharp pops echoed through the cavernous interior of the first floor.

"What in the hell was that?" Jason said, stopping on the steps and turning to listen.

Another burst of small explosions echoed down the stairwell.

"Sounds like firecrackers, Walter," Charlton said. "Probably nothing to worry about."

"Why in hell would anyone be playin' with firecrackers?"

"I'll take a look, if you want."

"No, you take Lois on down. I'll be there in a minute." He started back up the steps when a scream echoed from below. It went on and on, then there was another series of pops.

"That does it, by God," Jason shouted. He started down the stairs and disappeared around a corner, Charlton hurrying after him.

Charlton turned to tell his wife to wait where she was. He rounded the corner, just as two men rushed down a long hall, brandishing weapons. They were dressed in security uniforms, and Charlton ran toward them. "What's wrong?"

One of the guards grabbed Charlton and hustled him along the hall. The second continued toward the stairwell. Charlton tried to pull free. "Now listen," he said, "I'm a guest here. Get your hands off me."

The guard tightened his grip and dragged his prisoner down the hall, then turned right into a large, high ceilinged room, where three more guards stood against one wall, their weapons trained on Walter Jason, his wife and the Aldrettis.

"Walter," Charlton gasped. "what the hell is going on?"

"Please shut up," his captor growled. "Move against the wall, and no one will get hurt."

Charlton wanted to ask about his wife, then realized if he said nothing, she might be safe.

Edith Jason seemed unruffled, more annoyed than frightened.

Steven Aldretti scowled at the guards, keeping one arm around Rosalie's shoulders. "Do you mind telling us what's going on?" he asked.

He got no answer. The look on his face was proof he already knew what was happening, but wouldn't accept it until someone told him.

Charlton heard a scream from down the hall. "Lois!" he shouted, and started for the door. The guard let him go and Charlton started to run. A burst of gunfire narrowly missed him, ripping a line of ragged holes in the wall just to the left of the doorway.

"Please stay where you are," the guard said.

A moment later, another man, also dressed like a security guard, turned into the game room with Lois Charlton in tow. The man pushed her gently toward her husband.

The guards seemed content to wait.

A large man with a beard suddenly appeared in the doorway. He looked at them quietly for a long moment, as if appraising them. He was on the heavy side, and conservatively dressed, almost Ivy League in his taste. He wore a tie with a loose Windsor, and a tweed sport coat under his rainwear. When he finally spoke, his voice was amazingly gentle and slightly accented.

"Ladies and gentlemen, I'm sorry for the inconvenience, but I'm afraid you'll have to come with us. I must ask you please to cooperate. If you do as you are told, you won't be harmed. We don't want to hurt any of you, but if you cause us to use force, you should know that we will do so. And without hesitation."

He studied them quietly for several seconds. As he was about to resume, a commotion in the hall distracted him. He turned toward the door just as the Charltons' chauffeur was shoved into the room.

The big man nodded pleasantly at the chauffeur, then directed him to join the other captives with a wave of his hand.

"We'll be leaving shortly. Naturally I can't tell you where we'll be going. Mr. Jason—" he nodded toward the host "—you shouldn't worry about your staff. We have taken care not to harm them. They have been cooperative and will be left alone as long as they continue to be so."

"What do you want with us?" Aldretti asked.

"That isn't the question, Mr. Aldretti. The question is, how much are you worth to us? And that is something we shall have to wait to discover, hmm?"

1

The building reeked of self-importance. Mack Bolan stopped at the foot of the broad stairway leading up through Doric columns and examined the imposing facade. He was used to this kind of show. Some of the more imposing buildings in Washington, D.C. were cast in the same mold. But he was expecting something sleek and modern, some faceless wall of glass and polished aluminum, as anonymous as the men who would work behind the walls.

The warrior climbed the stairs, looking up at the ornate limestone lintel of the enormous bronze-and-glass doors as he passed through. The lobby was cordoned off with a velvet rope on either side, funneling all entrants down to a surly-looking man behind a high walnut counter.

Bolan stopped in front of the deskman. The Executioner was a big man and rested his elbows on the edge of the counter. The clerk noticed the black-clad arms and looked over his spectacles with silent disapproval.

"Major Radiguet, please."

"Is he expecting you?"

"Yes, he is."

"Your name?"

Bolan told him, then waited while the clerk turned away and whispered into a telephone. When he turned back, he looked no more hospitable, but his expression suggested the least little bit that he was impressed. "Someone will be right down." He pointed toward a leather settee, and Bolan drifted over to it and sat.

Two minutes later, a young man in a black turtleneck and blue jeans materialized behind the velvet cord, spoke briefly to the clerk, then moved toward Bolan with a smile that appeared to be genuine if somewhat reserved.

As he drew closer, he extended his hand. Bolan stood and took it as the young man said, "Lieutenant Michel Martell, Mr. Belasko. Direction de la Surveillance du Territoire. You know the DST?"

Bolan noticed the firm grip and shook the offered hand briskly. "DST is counterespionage, right?"

"Among other things, yes. Your Mr. Stiles is waiting upstairs. Major Radiguet and I will fill you in." He kept talking as he led Bolan past the desk, down a long marble-floored hallway to a bank of elevators, which was flanked by a row of call buttons. Martell pushed 4 and stood back to wait for the car.

"How much have you been told, Mr. Belasko?"

"Only that some American citizens have been kidnapped."

"We'll tell you whatever we can, but I'm afraid it's not much."

"I've worked with less than that," Bolan said. Martell laughed, but stopped when he realized that the American wasn't joking.

The elevator arrived, giving the young man a chance to regain his composure. Once inside, neither man spoke. When the car stopped at the fourth floor, Martell stepped out, keeping one hand on the door until Bolan stepped into the corridor.

"This way," Martell said, moving to the left and heading toward the front of the building. Great arched windows at the end of the corridor filled the high-ceilinged hall with bright white light.

Martell picked up his pace, and Bolan followed along in the lieutenant's wake. Turning left, they walked down a second, narrower corridor, stopping moments later in front of an open door. Martell gestured for Bolan to precede him, and closed the door before taking the lead again.

An inner office behind a closed door was their destination. Martell rapped on the glass, then walked in. Two men were seated at a long oval table. Martell introduced his superior, Claude Radiguet. The major was a sour-looking man with a thin face and a bushy mustache. His gray eyes took Bolan in, but his face remained immobile, even when he introduced his companion, Addison Stiles, an aide to the American ambassador to France.

Stiles nodded, stood to shake Bolan's hand, then dropped back into his chair. "I think we better get right to it, Major Radiguet."

Radiguet apparently agreed, because he gestured for Bolan to sit. "You know why you're here, do you not?"

"Yes."

"Very well. Michel, please give Mr. Belasko the background on our little . . . situation."

Martell took a seat across from Radiguet and turned to Bolan. "Two days ago seven Americans were kidnapped. There was a small party at the home of Walter Jason, a former American ambassador. Jason and his wife, as well as four guests and the chauffeur of one of the couples, were abducted at gunpoint. Three security guards were killed, and two more are missing."

"Presumed dead?" Bolan asked.

"We're not sure. There is at least a chance that they were part of the team of terrorists who conducted the raid."

"Are you sure they're terrorists? Jason is a very wealthy man. It could have been a kidnapping for ransom."

"I'll get to that. We have already received communication from the kidnappers. There is no doubt that it was politically motivated. There are demands, of course."

"There always are," Bolan said.

"And those demands suggest that whoever is responsible for the abduction has a very serious political agenda. And they have very detailed knowledge of a certain political situation in eastern Europe."

"Don't glamorize the pigs, Michel," Radiguet interrupted. "They are thugs, nothing more."

"You seem to know who we're talking about, Major," Bolan said.

"It is my business to know such things, Monsieur Belasko. And I am very good at my business."

"I don't doubt it."

Martell watched his superior, waiting for some indication that he could resume. Radiguet glared at Bolan a moment, then nodded to his underling.

"The communication we received identifies the responsible group as the Armenian People's Struggle."

"Never heard of them."

"It is a fairly new organization," Martell replied, "less than a year old, as far as we know. There has always been a kind of ferment in émigré politics in France, as I'm sure you know. The Armenians have been particularly active in recent months. There are many groups. They come and go, break up and reform. This particular organization seems to have arisen from the ashes of another."

"Organization?" Radiguet snorted. "It is a band of outlaws, nothing more. And not a very successful one at that."

"Successful enough to kidnap seven people in one fell swoop," Stiles suggested.

"A fluke, an accident. These men are fools. You will see that very soon."

"Look, Major Radiguet, why don't we finish the briefing? You can editorialize after we have all the facts." Bolan stared the major down, and after a long pause, Radiguet nodded to Martell.

The lieutenant seemed a little reluctant, as if he were glad the major had been brought to heel, but didn't wish to be so transparent that Radiguet would notice. He fiddled with some papers in an open folder. Clearing his throat, he said, "The seven people who were kidnapped are Walter Jason, whom I've already mentioned, and his wife Edith, Steven Aldretti, who was attached to NATO in Brussels at the same time Jason was ambassador, and Aldretti's wife Rosalie, and Norman and Lois Charlton, along with their chauffeur, a man named David Henderson."

"Do you have any idea why these people were getting together?"

"I'm sorry. I don't know what you mean."

"Was it a business meeting, purely social, what? Is there any reason they were preferred choices for kidnapping? Did Jason or Aldretti have any history with this Armenian group?''

Martell shook his head. "We're looking into all that, but right now we just don't know. At the moment it doesn't appear as if any of those abducted were targeted for any reason other than convenience. There is no grudge involved, in other words, as far as we have been able to learn.''

Stiles tapped his hand nervously on the table. "Look, Belasko, all that is beside the point. We want those people back, and we want it done quickly. We can't have every damn lunatic group in the universe targeting American citizens. Just find them and get them back.''

Bolan had no patience for the kind of bullheaded approach Stiles was advocating. It was men like him, Bolan knew, who made Americans targets in the first place. They swaggered across the planet like drunken conquerors, their arrogance so obvious and so irritating, that all Americans were tarred with the same brush.

"Stiles, in my experience there is often some sort of link, something that binds the kidnapper and the kidnapped together. Not always, but often enough that it is worth exploring. I want to know as much as I can learn about Jason and the others. If you want these people back alive, you'll just have to let me do it the right way. Not *your* way.''

"Who do you think you're talking to, Belasko? You can't—"

Bolan stood. "I can. You want this done right, get out of my way and let me do it. Otherwise, find somebody else."

"But—"

Martell, anxious to smooth things over, raised a hand. "Gentlemen, perhaps it would be useful if I was to play the tape now." He glanced at Radiguet, who shook his head.

The lieutenant stood and walked to the other end of the table. He clicked on the tape deck and turned up the volume. After several seconds of a loud hissing noise, the volume dropped, they heard the sharp rap of the microphone hitting something, possibly a tabletop, then a resonant baritone in accented English. "The Armenian People's Struggle demands the release of the following political prisoners—Vartan Vartanian, David Vartanian, Rumig Barok..." The list droned on, finally totaling twenty-three people. Bolan raised a hand.

Martell leaned over to stop the tape as the Executioner asked, "Do you know who all these people are?"

"We do, they are all—"

Radiguet interrupted. "They are all felons, all in prison where they belong."

"French prisons?" Bolan asked.

"Of course, French prisons."

"Can you release them?"

"Out of the question!"

Bolan shook his head. "I don't mean will you, but do you have the authority?"

"Yes, but—"

"To whom was the tape sent, Major? Was it sent to you directly?"

"Yes. Why do you ask?"

"I just want to know everything that might be significant."

Martell turned the tape back on. The melodious baritone continued. "We have taken seven hostages. Walter Jason among them. I'm sure you know who the others are, by now. If the Armenian patriots are not released, the hostages will never be seen again. For the moment they are unharmed. I wish that to remain the case, but that is up to you."

The voice stopped. A click, where recording had stopped, signaled the return of the blank tape hiss.

Bolan leaned back in his chair. "All right, Lieutenant, tell me everything you know about the Armenian People's Struggle."

Radiguet clucked in disgust. "I already told you. Thugs, nothing more."

"Major, maybe it would be best if Lieutenant Martell and I spent some time on this. Why don't you and Mr. Stiles go have lunch and meet us here again at two o'clock."

Radiguet nearly exploded. "Are you—"

"He's right, Major," Stiles soothed. "Let Martell get him up to speed. We don't have to be here for that." He grabbed Radiguet by the arm and tugged him toward the door. The major left, glaring over his shoulder at Bolan until Stiles finally closed the door.

Martell smiled, then let out a sigh of relief. "I don't know how you managed that, but it's a damn good thing you did."

"We have work to do," Bolan said. "Start talking."

2

The intel Martell had provided was minimal, and the pieces didn't hold together all that well. It was like being handed a bag full of jigsaw-puzzle pieces and told it was complete. The DST was conscious of its second-rate status behind the CIA and MI-6, but the French self-image wouldn't allow that to be publicly acknowledged. Martell didn't seem like a bad sort, but he didn't bring a whole hell of a lot to the table.

That meant that Mack Bolan was on his own. As usual.

One man worth investigating, according to Martell's sources, was Savoog Hampirian. He was somewhat of a mystery—part professor of history at the University at Nantes, part political theorist and part terrorist, if one could believe what one could trawl out of the deep and dark waters of the Armenian underground. One threw out a net and hauled in everything, then dumped the seine on the deck and sorted through the mess, chucking away ninety-five percent of what came up.

The Armenians had been perennial victims. So traumatized by the Turks in 1915, a slaughter in which uncounted millions died, the survivors had turned on one another like sharks in a feeding frenzy, tearing themselves to pieces while the rest of the world stood by amazed at such brutality.

But times were different. The lead blanket of Soviet control was gone. If the bomb went off now, it would do more than rattle a few worthless windows. It could be a shooting war. And the problem with all newly muscled political factions was their unpredictability. Jockeying for position, men who would be leaders resorted to tactics they would otherwise deplore. Nothing was more important than getting out ahead of the pack and staying there. It was the only way to avoid being trampled in the stampede.

Hampirian was out front, maybe not the frontrunner, but close to it. At least that was the word. When asked how accurate his information was, Martell had shrugged. "Your guess is as good as mine."

So, it was square one. The first order of business was to check out an address Martell had given him. It was a tenement on Rue de Balzac that Hampirian, for some reason, was known to frequent. Martell had tried to get someone inside, but had come up empty. Bolan meant to do better.

After cruising past the building twice and making a circuit of the block, Bolan parked his rented car three blocks away. It was the kind of neighborhood even muggers would avoid after dark.

The streetlights were few, and half of them weren't working. The stubs of shattered bulbs dangled filaments into the damp air. Vandals, or residents, had broken the white glass globes and the bulbs inside them to keep light at bay. Newspapers still damp with the rain, curled loose and tried to peel off the pavement with every gust of wind.

In the gutters, clogged with garbage, water trickled in a shallow stream. Most of the buildings were as dark as the street itself. Even the sounds of the night were muted. Distant traffic, an occasional horn, the rumble of a train, everything was muffled by the humid air.

With a block to go, Bolan took cover in a doorway. He could see the building now, and wanted to watch it for a few minutes before moving closer. Nothing differentiated the building from the rest of the tenements on the block. It was just as dark, its front just as grimy, its paint as cracked and windows as dirty.

The Executioner moved out of the doorway as a flash of sheet lightning threw the narrow street into momentary relief. A few minutes later he stood directly across from the tenement. Looking up, he saw a single light burning on the fourth floor. The warrior crossed the street, and entered a narrow alley beside the stairs and ducked into the shadows.

According to Martell, Hampirian's visits took him to the fifth floor. No one knew who he visited or why. No one knew that it was politics that brought the portly historian to the building, but if there was a logical explanation, that had to be it.

Bolan moved down the alley to the back of the building. A fire escape zigzagged down the back of the tenement. The ladder was high off the ground, but it didn't matter. He just wanted to get the layout clear in his mind before going in the front way. On the fifth floor, five windows arranged in two pairs with a single between them, spread across the width of the building. A narrow yard, with a high wooden fence of bare wood enclosing it, ran slightly downhill toward the rear of a similar tenement on the next block.

He went back up the alley to the street. Taking the steps one at a time, he opened the front door. Inside a vestibule that stank of cabbage, he looked at the mailboxes. Most had no names, only apartment numbers. The two boxes for the fifth floor were anonymous.

The inner door was closed, but when he tried the knob, it swung open easily. The strike plate was missing from the door frame, and a dead bolt protruded from the door like a thick, rude tongue. A chunk of the frame was missing where the dead bolt would have secured the door. The stairs were wide, as if to compensate for the narrowness of the building and the hallway that stretched beyond them.

As the warrior climbed, he stopped to listen occasionally. At each landing he checked behind him, then peered up the well to the railing of the next flight. On the second-floor landing, a small circular fluorescent light flickered, trying to catch and hold. It pinged with every flicker but offered only a dim, blue-tinged light.

By the time Bolan reached the fifth floor, he was prepared to find nothing of value. There were two apartments, but the door to the second was in a small hall off the main corridor. According to Martell, Hampirian visited the rear apartment.

Moving down the sticky hallway floor, the Executioner stopped a few feet from the turn leading to the rear apartment. Getting inside might be difficult. He couldn't just walk up and ring the bell, if it even worked. Kicking the door in might get him some trouble he couldn't afford. The only other option was to pick the lock and go in like a burglar. It wasn't something the warrior preferred to do, but any port in a storm.

He reached into his pocket for a set of lock picks, held them in his left hand and drew the Beretta. Ears alert for any sound in the stairwell or the hallway behind him, Bolan moved into the tiny alcove. He stopped in his tracks—the door was open.

The Executioner pocketed his lock picks and shifted the fire control on the Beretta to tri-burst. From somewhere inside the darkened apartment he heard a whispered conversation. He listened to the voices for a moment, trying to hear what they were saying. The tone was low and the language guttural.

While Bolan decided his next move, a circular swatch of light darted across the floor, hit a wall, then moved to the left, where it stopped on a door. A person didn't walk around his own apartment with a flashlight. Whoever was inside was as much a stranger to the place as the Executioner was.

Bolan slipped through the doorway and flattened against the wall before slipping behind the open front door. The light grew brighter and he heard footsteps now.

The man with the flashlight moved to the door, the circle of illumination contracting as it grew brighter. A second man was right behind the first. Both carried weapons—one an Uzi, the other an automatic pistol.

Bolan shifted his grip on the Beretta. The man with the light stepped to one side to allow his companion to open the door, which swung open with a bang. The flashlight was aimed through the doorway while the men crouched, guns ready. Apparently the room was empty, because both men relaxed a little and went in.

Bolan slipped out from cover and cat-footed across the room to stand beside the open doorway. Weird shadows danced on the floor as both men inside moved around the room. The warrior heard the scrape of wood on wood, as if someone were opening and closing drawers. The men were conducting a search of some kind. He wished to hell he knew what they were looking for, but the muttered conversation was meaningless to him.

They were getting angry, though. One drawer was ripped out and its contents scattered on the floor.

Shifting the Beretta to his left hand, Bolan snaked his arm around the door frame and groped for a light switch. He found it, counted to three and clicked it on. A stunned silence lasted for a split second.

One of the men shouted, and bolted through the doorway. The Executioner waited as the man started to turn and his companion left the bedroom. "Don't move," Bolan barked. "Drop your weapons."

The man with the pistol complied. He was framed in the light from the next room. His accomplice was partly in darkness. Maybe it was that partial security, or the false sense of invulnerability the Uzi gave him, but he didn't listen.

Bolan saw the movement and snapped a quick burst. The three 9 mm slugs slammed into his chest, and the guy squeezed off a short burst from the Uzi as he sank to the floor. The other gunner dived for his own weapon, and Bolan fired again, three more slugs plowing into the floor just ahead of the reaching hand. The warrior kicked the automatic away.

"Get up," he growled.

The man looked up at him, his eyes wide, as if he expected to be blown away. When Bolan waved with the Beretta, the gunner nodded. He got to his hands and knees, then bowed his body like a sprinter in the blocks.

As he straightened, he took off, knocking the Beretta to one side as he barreled past Bolan and at the door. The light went off and the door slammed. The Executioner pivoted, kicked the door open just as the man dived through the window and onto the fire escape, landing on his shoulder and rolling against the restraining rail. But it gave way, and the gunner clawed at the edge of the steel platform for a moment as his weight carried him over. His hands scratched at the metal for another second, but there was nothing to grab on to. Then he was gone.

Bolan raced back to the other room, closed the front door and flicked on the main light. Searching the dead man, he found nothing—no wallet, no license, no ID of any kind. He used the phone to call Michel Martell, then started to search the place. The apartment was dirty and sparsely furnished. He found nothing in either of the two bedrooms. Whatever the two men had been looking for, it apparently wasn't here.

Back in the main room, he sat on a wooden chair to wait for Martell. On the floor beside the dilapidated sofa, he spotted a handbag, which looked out of place. He got up from the chair and walked over to pick it up. Inside, he found a wallet, several kinds of makeup, some tissues and a key ring that held a key to a Mercedes.

He opened the wallet, flipped to the plastic windows and found himself staring at the face of Lois Charlton.

At least one of the hostages had been here. But where was she now? And just what was Savoog Hampirian's involvement?

3

While he waited for Martell, Bolan went over the apartment with a fine-toothed comb. After a half hour of searching, the Frenchman still hadn't arrived, and the only thing Bolan had found was the purse belonging to Lois Charlton.

He was beginning to think he was barking up the wrong tree. A dozen explanations for the purse presented themselves, but none was very credible. It could have been stolen at some other time, maybe in a mugging. But when he picked through its contents, he found a datebook bearing entries as recent as the day of the kidnapping. So there could be no other explanation. It had been in Lois Charlton's possession until she was abducted. So why was it sitting there on the floor?

It had to mean she had been there, or at least that her kidnappers had been there. But why just the one bag? Had it been left on purpose, maybe by Charlton herself or by someone who was trying to sabotage the terrorists?

A knock on the apartment door interrupted the warrior's thoughts.

Bolan drew the Beretta and eased the door open. Martell stood there for a moment, then stepped past Bolan and walked into the apartment.

"What happened?"

The warrior closed the door before replying. "I came to have a look at this place. When I got upstairs, the door was open. Two men were tossing the place."

"Tossing?"

"Searching. I tried to capture them, but things got out of hand. I shot one, and the other fell off the fire escape. He's in the yard out back."

"Let's take a look," Martell looked past Bolan at the body on the floor, then stepped closer. Dropping to one knee, he leaned forward to see the face more clearly in the dim light. He shook his head. "I don't know this man."

Martell started to go through the dead man's pockets, but Bolan stopped him. "I already checked. There's no ID, nothing at all."

"What about the other man?"

Bolan shrugged.

"You wait here, then. I'll be right back." Martell straightened and walked out. The Executioner walked to the back room. Three minutes later, he saw the beam of a flashlight pick its way around the corner and into the yard.

Outlined in the stark light, Bolan could see the splayed arms and the torso of the second gunman. Martell knelt beside the body, then rolled it over and expertly went through one pocket after another. He found something in a hip pocket, probably a wallet, tucked it into his coat, then finished his search and clicked off the light. As if in an afterthought, he clicked the light on again and played the beam on the face for a few seconds. The light was then clicked off. Moments later Martell joined the Executioner.

"Never saw him before, either," the lieutenant reported. "I found a wallet, though." He reached into his pocket and pulled out the small leather wallet and opened it.

Squatting, he removed the contents and spread it out on the floor—money, both French and American, but not much; a business card in a language Bolan assumed was Armenian, and a matchbook cover. Not much.

Martell turned the matchbook cover over in his hand once, then again. He leaned closer as if looking for something, maybe a penciled note or a phone number, but there was nothing other than the printed logo and name and address of a place called Café Americaine.

"The name mean anything to you?" Bolan asked.

"Yes. It's very well-known to us. A place where political types hang out. Refugees from a dozen countries, expatriates from your country and half the countries of Eastern Europe meet to share their mutual dissatisfaction with the way the world is.''

"Including Armenians?"

"Yes," Martell replied, "including Armenians."

"But you don't recognize either of the dead men?"

"Never saw either of them before. I thought we knew pretty much all there was to know about the Armenian People's Struggle. Now I'm not so sure."

"So we're right where we started."

"Not quite."

"There is someone who might be able to help us. She is someone who might know who these men are."

"Then bring her in and let her take a look."

"It's not that easy."

"Why not?"

"I don't want to go into that. Just believe me that we can't do it. She's done some work for me in the past, but I don't know where she lives. I've tried to find out, but she spotted the tail I put on her and told me that if it happened again, she'd be through working for me. She was too useful to lose."

"If you don't know how to contact her, what good is she?"

"She frequents the Café Americaine."

"Then let's go talk to her."

"I can't. If she saw me there, she'd probably run." Martell smiled. "But she might talk to you."

"Why me?"

"Just a feeling I have."

"Who is she?"

"Her name is Anna Chirkizian. She knows every Armenian on the planet, it seems. As near as I've been able to learn, her family was influential in the local Communist Party in Armenia. Then something happened, but I don't know what. She came to France, but she has stayed in touch with developments back home. It's almost as if she has her own network. Maybe she does, for all I know. But she's worth talking to. More than half of what I know about Armenian émigré politics I got from Anna."

"It seems there's another half missing, doesn't it?"

Martell tilted his head to one side. "Maybe so. Things change fast. With what's going on in Armenia lately, they will probably change a lot faster now."

"You trust this woman?"

"Not completely, no. But she's never lied to me, at least as far as I have been able to determine."

"I don't like it."

"I don't, either. But in my business, I have to do many things I don't like. People like Anna are often the only source of information. Often they have a personal agenda, some reason they do what they do. But a man in my position can't be too particular where he finds what little help there is."

"So I just walk up to her and tell her you sent me. Is that how it works?"

"Not quite. But I will give you a code she will recognize."

"How much do I tell her?"

"You'll have to use your own judgment, Mr. Belasko. Once you make contact with her, we'll have to be extremely careful. She is extremely suspicious, but she seems to trust me, or at least to find me useful often enough that she has maintained our somewhat tenuous relationship for three years now."

Bolan wasn't convinced.

"You know, the next step will be some sort of deadline for the release of the Armenian prisoners. I don't know how much time we have, but I know that things will start to move quickly sometime soon. When that happens, we will not have very much control. If you're not going to talk to Anna, then we have to find some other approach."

"What you're saying is that there *is* no other approach, isn't that right?"

Martell took a deep breath. "Not exactly. What I'm saying is that Anna Chirkizian is my most reliable source. I understand your reluctance to rely on her. She may, after all, be involved in this business. Maybe she engineered it, for all we know. But until I know I can't trust her, I have no choice but to do so."

Bolan let his breath out in an exasperated sigh. "All right. I'll do it. But at the first sign she's double-dealing, I'm walking away from her. Do you understand?''

Martell nodded.

"What about this mess here?'' Bolan waved a hand to take in the apartment.

"I'll take care of it. I'll get you an ID on these men as soon as I can, but I don't know how long it will take. Some of these people are here for years without finding their way into the records. I don't know whether we'll be able to learn much, but I'll try."

"How do I contact you, once I see her?"

Martell scribbled a phone number on a page from his pad. Tearing it off the pad, he handed it to Bolan and said, "That's my home number. Try not to use it, but if you have to, I'll get the message. Otherwise I'll meet you at your hotel. You can also get a message to me through Anna Chirkizian."

4

Bolan took a cab to the Montparnasse district. It was home to a hundred varieties of artistes, charlatans, phonies and poseurs. Poets by the dozens, some of whom could actually write, haunted the bars and cafés, painters and fakes with paint-spattered clothes haunted the all-night lounges listening to jazz and to one another talk about how the philistines failed to recognize their talent for yet another year.

Booze flowed freely in Montparnasse and dope was cheap. Hookers draped themselves over anybody who looked like he might have two francs to rub together. Bolan hated it all—the smell of the bars, the cheap perfume that hung in the dark air like a noxious cloud, the cigarette smoke that turned white faces blue and painted faces gray, the loud music and the loudmouthed frauds. But he was looking for someone, and when you wanted to find someone badly enough, you went where that person lived.

He didn't know for sure where to find Anna Chirkizian, but he knew the kind of places she was most likely to frequent. Martell had said his best bet was Café Americaine, and he would start there. He walked along the cluttered streets, so old they weren't wide enough to accommodate cars two abreast. Papers curled in the gutters and skittered across the wet pavement on a stiff breeze as he moved down Rue de Chambord and ducked into the establishment known as Café Americaine.

Inside, a loud band featuring an overmiked tenor sax was cranking out a mixture of R and B and juke-joint jazz. The place was packed, and Bolan had to squeeze past a fair number of people to reach a table in the corner, then squeeze into a chair wedged against the wall.

A waitress in a shiny skirt and black leotard noticed him and threaded her way through the crowd, holding her tray perpendicular to the floor, following it as it sliced like a buzzsaw through the throng.

The band finished one number, leaving a sudden sonic vacuum so that her voice sounded like a shout when she asked what he wanted. The Boston accent was unmistakable. He wondered if he was that easily made as an American that she would have used English right off the bat, then realized no reasonable Frenchman would be caught dead in a place with that name.

"A beer," he said. She nodded and disappeared, trailing a cloud of a scent unexpectedly subtle. He saw her shimmy and shake her way to the bar, give his order, then stand to one side, popping her fingers in time to the next number. The beat was solid, the backbeat funky, and the guitarist actually wasn't bad.

The waitress materialized out of the wall of sound. He noticed her face was painted with something phosphorescent that picked up black light from somewhere. It seemed to float like a disembodied ghost until she got a little closer, when her shape was discernible against the undulating background of the dancers.

She carried the beer high to flatten her profile and minimize the resistance to her passage, the glass upended on the bottle. It was probably rattling, but there was too much noise to be sure.

Setting the bottle on the scarred table, she flipped her checkbook open, tilted it and said, "Five francs."

Bolan shook his head, slipping a larger note across the battered wood. She snatched it with a practiced flick of her wrist. "Anything else?"

"Yeah, as a matter of fact, there is. I'm looking for somebody."

"Honey, we're all looking for somebody. Even me. But I'm particular, you know what I mean?"

"So am I."

"Don't knock it unless you've tried it."

"That's not what I'm looking for."

"Hey, I don't know anything about drugs, so if that's what you mean, ask somebody else."

"No, I'm looking for a woman, but not the way you think."

"If there's another way, I haven't heard about it." She smiled then, to let him know she was teasing. Bolan didn't smile back. He didn't have time for fun and games, no matter how harmless.

Then, remembering she had no way of knowing that, he said, "Her name's Anna Chirkizian. She used to work here, I think. You know her?"

"I've heard of her, but I never actually met her. I can ask Lloyd, if you want."

"Who's Lloyd?"

"The manager. You want me to check for you?"

"Thanks."

"And who do I say is looking for her?"

"You don't."

"Hey, look, I don't know you from Adam. If I was her, and some guy comes looking for me, I gotta ask myself would I want my address handed out. And I think there's no way I'd want it. You know what I mean?"

Bolan nodded. She was right. But his name wouldn't mean anything to Lloyd. It wouldn't mean anything to Anna Chirkizian, either. If they called her to check, it might spook her, make her even harder to find. "Maybe I should talk to Lloyd myself."

"Lloyd doesn't talk to strangers. Hell, he hardly talks to employees."

"Let me worry about that."

"Anyplace I should send the body?" She smiled again, but this time it didn't seem like she was kidding.

"There won't be any body. Trust me on that. Where's Lloyd now?"

"In his office, probably. To the left of the bandstand. But don't think you're getting back there. That's what Garth is for."

"Garth's the bodyguard, I take it."

"You could say that. When you go past the bandstand, if you hit a wall covered with Ban-Lon, that'll be Garth."

"What's your name?"

"Charlene McGarrity. But I never told you anything. Not even Lloyd's name."

"I'll remember that."

Bolan watched her glide back into the crowd and disappear. He sipped his beer while the band continued its assault on silence, doing a shuffling version of an old Charlie Parker tune.

Bolan waited for the guitarist to start his solo, then squeezed out from behind the table and started to make his way toward the bandstand. It was tough going.

He earned a couple of hard stares and took one bony elbow in the ribs before reaching the left-hand corner of the dance floor, then eased past the bandstand into the relatively empty foyer from which a narrow corridor lighted with red bulbs led to the rear.

Bolan had just started down the corridor when a door opened at the far end. The man who stood before him had to be Garth. The guy was somewhere around six-six, and weighed in at about two-fifty. The Ban-Lon shirt stretched across his massive chest like a second skin.

Garth shook his head. "Don't be coming down here, pal."

"I'd like to see Lloyd."

"Lloyd wouldn't like to see you."

"How do you know, unless you ask?"

"I'm paid to know, not to ask."

"Maybe you're overpaid."

"Maybe you're out of your league, pal." They met about halfway down the hall. Garth reached out with one muscle-bound arm, his fingers already curling in expectation of closing over Bolan's shirt. But the Executioner was too quick for him. He slid in under the arm, caught it on the way by and jerked it up tight against Garth's back.

The bouncer started to protest, but Bolan jacked up the leverage a little, bringing the arm up until another fraction would make something pop. Through gritted teeth, Garth said, "You better not let go, pal. Ever."

Bolan pushed the arm a little higher. "Garth, all I want is to talk to Lloyd. I'm not looking for trouble, and I'm not interested in making any. Now, we can have it one of two ways. You either walk away and do your job, or you get hurt. However it goes down, I see Lloyd. What's it going to be?"

"All right, all right. Let go of my arm."

The warrior did, and Garth made a mistake. He turned and went for Bolan, who was expecting the move. Chopping down on both collarbones, he poleaxed the bodyguard, who went to his knees. The job was finished with a quick right cross that cracked like a hammer on granite. The impact sent a jolt up Bolan's arm, but Garth slumped against the wall and didn't move.

The Executioner wasn't even breathing hard. He moved down the hall to the black-painted door. Rather than knock, he turned the knob and walked in, finding himself in a cluttered office that appeared to be deserted. A second door was set in the wall to the right. He walked over and turned the knob. Locked. Another blind alley. The warrior headed for the main door and was about to go back down the corridor past Garth, when he heard a noise. The knob rattled on the locked door and he turned back as it swung open.

A woman stood on the threshold. She was tall and dark, and held a small automatic pistol in her hand.

"Who are you?" she asked. "What are you doing in here?"

"Looking for someone."

"Who?"

"Lloyd."

"Lloyd's not here."

"Do you work for him?"

"My name is Anna, and no, I don't work for him. As a matter of fact, he works for me."

"Maybe you can help me."

5

Savoog Hampirian watched the television with his head cocked to one side. He drummed his fingers on the arm of the threadbare sofa. He hated television, and he hated television news even more, because he knew it was nothing more than bad fiction, soap opera for international-affairs junkies. It was worse in the U.S., but it was like a cancer, spreading across the globe. Talking heads mouthed platitudes, spouted party lines, affected concern for the occasional human-interest story. The newscasters had become substitutes for court jesters. They made every man a king, with a fool of his own.

But this night was different. This night he expected to have reason to watch, because the people he had kidnapped were important. Not only that, but they were Americans, which made them even more important, at least in their own minds, and in that part of Europe that measured itself against the U.S., either aspiring to surpass it, or pretending to despise it. But what difference did it make whether you tried to be just like your enemy or tried so hard to be un-like him that you forgot who you were?

That was why he had taken Americans, after all. He wanted to be known as a serious man. He wanted the Armenian People's Struggle to be taken seriously. No one noticed you in the gutter. You had to reach out with a scabrous hand and haul someone down there with you to get his attention. Well, he had done that. Now, all that remained was to demonstrate just *how* seriously he meant to be taken.

He knew it might require bloodshed to make his point, and that was too bad. He had nothing against his captives, but there was a price to be paid for celebrity, one not always exacted. But when the bill came due, it had to be paid. And for the seven people now under his control, the bill was very close to coming due.

It might have been better to take Frenchmen. He was in Paris, after all. But nobody really cared about the French. They thought so much of themselves, that no one else cared to think of them at all. No, it was better to go where the money was, and the power. That meant Washington, and he couldn't expect the Americans to care about anyone but their own.

There was some nonsense on the screen now, something about Russia's blueprint for the future. Hampirian watched with a jaundiced eye, his hand on the remote control, waiting for an excuse to turn up the sound. But when the Russians were gone, there was a flickering gray interlude before new faces appeared.

On and on it went, one meaningless story after another, one pasty face after another. And then the news was over. It was over, and there had been no mention at all of the captured Americans. Two days. They had the tape by now. And there was no mention. His first reaction was rage. How dared they ignore him, how dared they ignore what he was trying to do? Millions of people were counting on him, and the world wasn't even listening.

When the rage subsided, he started to laugh. He didn't exist. That's what they were trying to tell him—he didn't exist. And if he didn't exist, then neither did the millions of others just like him. They were nonpersons. In the modern world, if you were beneath the notice of the unblinking eye of television, you were a cipher, a nonentity.

Then the laughter died away. He sat there for a long time, the remote control in his lap, the screen flickering as one image was swallowed by another, one long, meaningless squiggle of light and color. Soon he reached down to his lap and pressed the power switch on the remote. He heard the soft click, and the picture died with one last burst of white light.

He stared at the blank screen. With a long sigh he placed the remote on the coffee table next to the cup and saucer.

Things were different now. He had tried to play by the established rules, and the other side had taken the ball and gone home. So he would have to change the rules. He would force them to notice, to listen and, finally, to act.

But how?

Options were difficult to see for a man who had never had the luxury of choosing anything. The possibilities were endless for him now, and that was worse than having no choice at all. He needed something that would make them take him seriously, the French, the Americans, whoever would have to deal with him in the end. There was a danger in going too far, he knew that. But he also knew there was a danger in not going far enough. If you did that, they took you for a clown.

He was wise in the ways of the world. He remembered the attack on the Rome airport. That was too much. Those people had gone too far. But he remembered, too, the kidnapping of an American general. That group hadn't gone far enough then. And this was a single elimination tournament. You couldn't afford to lose even once. There were no second chances. He would eventually decide what to do, then act on it. There would be no turning back.

Hampirian looked at the telephone. He was tempted to use it but knew he shouldn't. It was too risky. He got up and walked to the table. With a sudden jerk, he wrenched the phone wire out of the wall, felt it resist for a spilt second, then part with a sharp crack. He threw the phone across the room where it shattered like the pile of cheap plastic it was.

He went to the bedroom and found the gun, a Skorpion he had stolen from the armory at Erivan. The gun was bulky, and he didn't want the ugly lump under his coat.

He put the weapon in a zippered bag, then looked around the room, trying to remember if there was anything else he would need. But nothing occurred to him. He turned off the light and went to the front door of the apartment, pausing once to look at the rug. It was a perfect specimen of the weaver's art. He'd found it in a bazaar in Tashkent, but that was in another life. It was the only material thing in the world he really cared about. It would be a shame to lose it. He would just have to make sure he was careful, that he would be able to come home again.

Hampirian closed the door and locked it, stuck the key in his pocket and made his way to the street.

He tossed the bag into the back seat of his car. Soon he would have to be more cautious, look under the hood for a bomb, check under the seat for a detonator. Soon, but not yet. Not until he taught them he was a man with a cause.

The drive out of the city took more than an hour. He used it to put the finishing touches on his plan. It was all coming together now. It was economical, but dramatic. It said what he wanted said, and it did so in a way that was impossible to ignore.

When he reached the farm south of the city, he turned onto a narrow lane. Moments later the house came into view.

He coasted to a stop in front of the building, killed the engine and reached for his bag before getting out of the vehicle and heading toward the house. He spotted the dim glow of a cigarette. At this hour, it would be Haroun on guard duty. As he drew closer, he spotted the sentry among the trees to the left of the house. He waved, then went in through the back door.

Michael Ekizian was sitting at the kitchen table. "Everything all right?" he asked.

Hampirian nodded. "Fine."

"What did they say on the news?"

"Nothing."

"What?"

"Not a word. That's why I'm here. We have to do something. Do you still have the camera?"

Ekizian nodded.

"Get it."

"Now?"

Hampirian made a sound of disgust. Ekizian got up and stomped out of the room. Hampirian waited until he was back with the camera. "Get the chauffeur," he said.

Ekizian looked slightly bewildered. "You heard me," Hampirian snapped. "Get him."

He took off his coat and draped it over the back of a chair. He could hear voices in the basement, then footsteps on the wooden stairs. A moment later, the attaché's chauffeur stumbled through the doorway, Ekizian right behind him. The chauffeur looked frightened.

Hampirian nodded to him. "Don't worry," he said. "There is nothing to be worried about."

To Ekizian, he said, "Meet me in the barn. Bring the camera and the lights."

"What for?"

"Just do it."

"The lights are upstairs."

"Get them."

Hampirian grabbed the bag, opened it and took out the Skorpion. Waving it toward the door, he told the chauffeur to step outside, then directed him to the barn.

The Armenian stayed several paces behind the chauffeur, who stopped in front of the barn door, even though it was half-open.

Hampirian moved cautiously past his prisoner and reached inside to turn on the lights. Two naked bulbs flickered into life. "Come in," he barked.

He motioned for the chauffeur to accompany him toward a wooden partition, partially concealed by two bales of hay. Hampirian patted one of them and said, "Sit down."

"What's going on?"

"We are going to send a little message to the authorities. Nothing special. I want you to say a few words. We will tape it."

"What should I say?"

"Nothing much. Just something like, 'These men are serious. You must do as they say.' Just enough for them to understand that we are not fooling."

Ekizian appeared in the doorway. "Over here," Hampirian said. He moved a few paces away from the chauffeur. "Here, this is perfect."

Ekizian took the position and hoisted the camera to his shoulder. He looked through the viewfinder. "There's not enough light."

"That's why I wanted you to bring the other lights. Here, give them to me." He bent to pick up the light bar. "How do you turn them on?"

"The red toggle, on top."

Hampirian clicked it, and the barn was suddenly full of the harsh glare of portable floodlights. "Ready?"

Ekizian grunted. The chauffeur nodded. The whirr of tape started.

"These men are serious," the chauffeur said. "You must do what they say." He looked at Hampirian, who was shaking his head.

"Stop the tape and rewind it." To the chauffeur Hampirian said, "Louder. It must be clear."

The tape started again, and the chauffeur cleared his throat. "These men are serious. You must do what they say."

He looked at Hampirian and started to ask a question. The stuttering chatter of the Skorpion drowned it out.

"Perfect."

6

"What do you want with me?"

Bolan didn't answer right away. Instead he scrutinized the woman with such intensity that she blushed.

There was a lot to appraise. She was taller than he expected, maybe five-ten. And younger. He put her age in her late twenties. Long legs and a full bosom gave her the appearance of someone who might have modeled if she had chosen. Long black hair, which she wore straight and unadorned, draped her shoulders. Her full mouth, pale enough that he suspected she wore no makeup, was pursed in anger.

"When you are done drooling, perhaps you'd like to tell me who you are and what you want."

Her black eyes seemed to flash at him, but they held a trace of amusement.

"You're not what I expected," he said.

"Ah, I see. You expected something, did you? And just what was it that you expected?"

"I don't know."

"Perhaps an old hag shaped like a barrel with yellow hair and breasts drooping to her waist. Is that what you expected? A stereotype? Perhaps if I got a mop and a pail, put on my babushka, you would feel more comfortable."

Bolan admired the woman's direct manner, and she aroused his curiosity. But he knew it was more. Anna Chirkizian radiated an animal intensity, magnetism. And he found it appealing.

"Look," Anna said, "you went to a lot of trouble to meet me. You must have had a reason. I'm curious as to what it might have been."

He recited the password Martell had provided to him.

Her face grew dark then, the black eyes receding a little, almost as if they had withdrawn behind protective hoods. Her jaw stiffened and she turned away.

"Who are you?" she asked suddenly, whirling back to face him.

"What difference does that make?"

"It makes all the difference in the world."

"Someone who needs information. I need help, and I've been told that you might be able to provide it. My name is Mike Belasko, but that's not important."

"You're an American, aren't you."

It wasn't a question, but he nodded anyway.

"Then I know what you want. But I'm afraid I can't help you."

"Can't or won't?"

"There is no difference. In either case you get no help. Please leave."

"Or what? You'll call Garth?"

"I don't need Garth to protect me," she said. The gun in her hand had reappeared so suddenly, Bolan wasn't sure where she had concealed it. But it sat there comfortably. She wasn't afraid of it, and that meant she was not afraid to use it.

"So I see."

"Now, please, just leave me alone."

"What do you know about the Armenian People's Struggle?"

"Nothing."

"I don't believe you."

"You're a brave man. Do you always argue when a gun is pointed at you?"

"Only when I have reason to."

"And you have reason now, is that it?"

"I was told by someone I believe that you know everything there is to know about Armenian émigré politics in France. There's reason to believe that people involved in one of those groups have kidnapped seven American citizens. Now that's all the reason I need. If you know anything, I think you should seriously consider what it means if you don't tell me and something happens to those people."

"Those people are nothing to me. They are Americans. I mean nothing to them, and I am only too happy not to care what happens to them."

"If anything *does* happen to them, you could wind up in serious trouble."

"I have been in serious trouble all my life. It is nothing new. That is what it means to be an Armenian. I have gotten used to it, I suppose. In any case, I don't know anything, so there is nothing for me to worry about."

"I suppose you don't know Savoog Hampirian, either."

"I know him, yes." She was getting distracted, and the muzzle of the automatic was wandering a little. If it wandered enough, she just might give the warrior an opening.

"You know he's been singled out as one of those who could be responsible for the kidnapping, don't you?"

"I told you, I know nothing about the kidnappings."

"Fine."

Bolan made as if to move. He turned away and started toward the door. Then, as an afterthought, he turned back to face her. "Two people have already been killed. I wouldn't feel so safe if I were you. Maybe the next guy who comes looking for you won't be so easily discouraged."

"Security guards at Walter Jason's house. But the newspaper said there were three."

"No, I'm not talking about that. I mean tonight, at an apartment on Rue Balzac."

That shook her a little. He could tell she wanted to ask, but didn't know how.

"Sorry I bothered you, Miss Chirkizian," he said, turning away again.

"No, wait. These people. Who were they?"

"I don't know. Neither does DST. But they will."

"You killed them, didn't you?"

"One of them. The second guy fell off a fire escape."

"On Rue Balzac, you say?"

Bolan nodded.

"What address?"

"Two-forty-one. Top floor. Rear."

She rubbed her cheek with her free hand. The tip of her tongue darted out to moisten her dry lips. "Suppose I do know something? Then what?"

"Hypothetically?"

"Yes."

"That depends on what it is you know."

"Are you CIA?"

"No."

"And I'm supposed to believe you?"

"Then why did you ask? Would you believe me if I said yes?"

She shook her head. "I don't know why I asked. I just . . . I'm confused."

"That sounds like the first honest thing you've said tonight."

She smiled then. "Perhaps it is."

"Why don't you keep going. You're on a roll."

"I want to talk to someone. Maybe then I can tell you. I need time to think."

"We don't have time, Miss Chirkizian. We have to find those people alive. We don't even know how much time we have, but it won't be much."

"Sit down. I'll be right back."

"No. I'll leave a number where you can reach me if you change your mind. I don't have time to waste on playing games with you."

"No games. I'll be back in ten minutes. Maybe sooner."

"All right. Ten minutes. Any longer, and I won't be here when you get back."

She nodded, opened the door and left, leaving Bolan to sit and stare at the empty room. He didn't know why, but he thought he had detected a subtle change in the woman. Something seemed to have frightened her, as if his news had meant more than he understood.

Bolan glanced at his watch twice. The second time, it was closing on the ten-minute mark. He was starting to get to his feet when the door opened again. Anna Chirkizian was back. With her was a big rawboned man of about Bolan's age. He was dressed in jeans and a sweater, over which he wore an ancient trench coat. It glistened with moisture.

In the man's left hand was a Browning automatic. He pointed it at Bolan. "Who the hell are you? Anna says you've been leaning on her."

"If that's what she's told you, she's never been leaned on by anybody. Certainly not by me."

"What's all this about two men killed tonight?"

"Friends of yours?"

"No, of course not."

"Then why get involved?"

"Because I care about Anna. I don't want anybody coming around here and giving her a hard time."

"It seemed to me she could handle herself pretty well. I don't know why she felt she needed you."

"Look, mister, she doesn't have anything to say to you. Why don't you just leave her alone?"

"Because she might know something I need to know."

"You don't really think she had anything to do with those kidnappings. What else do you need to know?"

"I need to know who *did* have something to do with it, and I think she can help me there."

"No, she can't."

"So she said."

"But I can," Anna interrupted.

Both men looked at her. Bolan wondered why she'd changed her mind. The other man seemed to be wondering what other secrets she'd kept from him.

"I'll... All right. I'll help you as much as I can." She seemed to be breathing with some difficulty, as if the prospect of cooperating with the big American were some life-threatening compromise.

Maybe it was, Bolan thought.

7

Bolan and Anna's champion, whose name was Don Marshack, sat in the café. It was difficult to be heard over the music, but Marshack seemed to want to share his life story. He was a big man, probably six-one or -two, and went a solid 210. He wore his light brown hair long and sported a nasty Fu Manchu that was a little darker. His eyes were gray, but their piercing gaze suggested he saw things others didn't see. There was a scar on one cheek, an inch or so of it showing above the scraggly beard that seemed to have a mind of its own.

Marshack's past was eventful, to say the least. Bolan got it in bits and pieces—three years in Laos with Air America, a year in the Phoenix program, then five years in the Middle East. Marshack didn't seem to be tormented by his background as much as saddened by it. It sounded almost as if it had happened to someone else.

"So I quit," Marshack stated. "I had run out of steam, I guess. It felt like that, anyhow. Now I'm a painter. It's more logical. I feel in control. I paint when I want, and when I don't want to, I don't. Nobody tells me what to paint, and if they don't like what I do, they can screw themselves. It's better that way.''

He stopped to take a sip from his beer. Setting the glass on the table, he looked at Bolan for a long time, as if waiting for the warrior to share his own history. But the big guy stayed quiet.

Marshack wasn't ready to let it go at that. "Tell me about yourself, Belasko. Why do you care what goes on half a world away from your home?''

"It's what I do.''

Marshack snorted. "All right. Let's say I accept that. What do you want with Anna? Why do you think she can help you?''

"I was told she knew everything there was to know about Armenian émigré politics. I was also told it was a minefield, and that one needed a guide to keep from blowing himself up.''

"And you think Anna can do that for you?''

Bolan nodded.

Marshack scratched his neck. "Suppose she can. What's in it for her?''

"Nothing. Unless she would take some satisfaction in knowing that innocent people's lives have been saved.''

"You think she's a do-gooder then, or your source does?''

"I don't know what to think. I came to see her and while I wait for her to decide to tell me what she knows, I'm sitting here drinking warm beer with an escapee from the Lost Generation who thinks he's a painter."

Marshack laughed at the dig. "Thinks? I get any-where from ten to thirty thousand for one of my paintings. Not bad, if you ask me."

Marshack finished his beer. "I'll tell you what I'm going to do," he said, wiping some foam from his mustache. "I'm going to tell Anna I think she can trust you, and that she should help you. For now. But if she agrees, I'm going to work with you. Or else we don't have a deal. How's that sound?"

"It doesn't sound good. I don't need some over-the-hill thrill seeker tagging along, reliving his glory days."

"Take it or leave it."

"What's your interest in all this?"

"Anna. I'll look out for her interests. That's the only reason I want to go along. I know what I'm do-ing, and I won't get in your way. But I don't think you can do it without me, so it's your call."

Bolan nodded.

"All right. For the time being."

Marshack pushed his chair back and stood. "Good. I'll be right back. You wait here. Have an-other beer."

"No, thanks."

But Marshack was already working his way through the crowd to the back room. Bolan watched him disappear as the door to the room opened and closed.

The man reappeared moments later, moving past a chastened Garth, who stood flexing his impressive biceps to compensate for his recent embarrassment. Marshack took a detour to the bar, then continued toward the table, a beer mug in each hand.

"Anna says she'll go along," he reported as he reclaimed his chair.

"Why?"

"You know what they say about gift horses."

"Yeah, I do."

"Good, then let's get started. I have two possible addresses for us to check out." He slipped a piece of paper across the table. "The one on top is yours. I'll check the other one."

"What's the second address?" the warrior asked as he looked at the note.

"That's my studio. I'll meet you there at—" he glanced at his watch "—one o'clock. Top floor. You know where it is?"

"I'll find it."

"Look, one thing you have to know."

"What's that?"

"You find anybody there, don't get stupid. I've been watching these Armenians ever since I met Anna. You spook these guys, and we'll never find the other hostages. They'll panic. At best they'll move them. At worst..." He drew a thick finger under his chin. "Believe it. And if you jeopardize her life, I'll kill you. Understand?"

Bolan shook his head. "You should understand something, too, Marshack. I don't kill easily. And I'm not interested in getting into some macho 'I'm the king of the castle' contest. Not with you, and not with anybody else. I have a job to do, and I will do it. Believe *that*."

"Fair enough." The Armenian pushed back his chair and stood. Leaning forward, he said, "If you need weapons, whatever, let me know."

"Thanks, but I don't need anything."

"You need one thing, Belasko. You need luck, and lots of it."

Bolan watched Marshack leave, waiting until he'd been gone three or four minutes before getting to his feet.

The band was louder now, and it seemed as if the sound itself was pushing him toward the door. Outside, it was cold and overcast. He took a cab to his car, patting his pocket as he entered the vehicle to make sure he still had the slip of paper Marshack had given him.

The address was on the fringes of the Monmartre district across the Seine, and after he left the Boulevard Saint Michel, the traffic thinned. He was headed toward a section of Paris that was a working class area, where few people had cars. Not as run down as Rue Balzac, it was still depressing and gloomy. Tendrils of fog curled around the car as he turned into Rue Clement. The streets were narrow, parking permitted on only one side, but even so, there were plenty of parking places.

Bolan parked the car, climbed out and sauntered down the street. The buildings were neat. He found the address without difficulty, but getting close wasn't going to be easy. Like the other buildings on the block, it was tall and narrow, and lights burned in several windows. He watched the building for several minutes. A small sign at the head of the stone stairs read École d'Armenie, and the school seemed to occupy the ground floor only.

Moving into the lobby, he checked the residents' list, a hand-lettered sheet of white cardboard with penciled lines separating one name from another. He backed out onto the porch again and went down the stairs for a recon.

The Executioner entered an alley that ran the length of the building's right side. It was deserted, and he ducked under a wooden arch and into the darkness. The first floor was several feet above the street level. He could see lights in two windows, but they were positioned too high for him to peer into.

He debated whether to return the following day, when he could manufacture some plausible excuse to visit the school. He heard a click and tensed, then realized a light had been turned on in the basement. Two narrow bands of light spilled into the alley.

Bolan moved to the closer of them and got down on his hands and knees. A thick curtain hung inside the glass, but it met imperfectly, and he could see a little of the room inside. Bookshelves lined one wall, and a desk sat in the middle of the floor. No matter which way he positioned himself, he couldn't see any more. But it was apparent the basement belonged to the Armenian school as well as the first floor.

He moved to the next window. More books were visible and to the left, a doorway. He could see into the room beyond it, but he was looking at a wall. If Bolan moved his head slightly, he could see part of a mirror. He watched the glass, hoping to see something reflected there, but nothing moved, nothing was visible.

Someone appeared in the doorway, and the light in the room went out. A man carrying a tray moved along the row of shelves and disappeared.

The Executioner cursed softly, but there was nothing he could do. He was about to get up and leave when he heard voices in the back. He got to his feet and inched toward the rear of the building. The voices were speaking French, but he couldn't hear them well enough to know what they were saying. As he got closer, almost as if they sensed his presence, they switched to Armenian.

He listened for two minutes, but learned nothing. A garbage can rattled, then stopped, and the voices faded away. Another window was positioned to the right of the rear stairs. Checking the back door to make sure it was closed, he moved past the steps. Dropping to his knees, he peered into a small room.

The first thing the warrior noticed was the metal door, and to the left he could see part of what appeared to be a cot. He tried the window, but it was locked. The curtains were parted a little wider, but he still couldn't see enough of the small room. Then someone moved. He could hear faint voices, speaking in English.

"Walter," a woman said in a tremulous voice, "how long are they going to keep us in this awful place?"

"Not long, Edith. Not long. I'm sure that whatever they want will be given to them."

Bolan was tempted to break the window, but he couldn't. There was no way he could get Jason and his wife out.

But at least he knew where they were.

For now.

8

Marshack's studio was in an old building. The front was crumbling brick, and the stairs leading up to the ancient door scarred and nicked. The Executioner pressed the bell, and a sharp buzz exploded somewhere overhead. He heard the latch click open and pushed the door, expecting it to creak loudly, but it swung back easily.

Marshack was on the top floor, and an elevator was too much to expect. The stairs were steep and narrow. Bolan started up the first flight, his hand sticking to the banister railing and coming away gritty.

A single naked bulb burned on the first landing, dangling by its wires from the high ceiling. When he reached the landing, sand grated under his feet on the antique tile. The grout was long gone, and had been replaced with the grime of a century mixed with some detergent paste left over from the occasional mopping.

The next three flights were carbon copies. The air reeked with a variety of spices the warrior didn't recognize. The higher he climbed, the more exotic the fragrances. The fourth-floor bulb was out, and Bolan stopped to listen. In the narrow confines of the stairwell, a man was a perfect target. There was no place to go except up or down. If an assassin held his fire long enough, catching his target in the middle of the stairs, it was a guaranteed kill.

Bolan felt for his gun and rested his palm on the butt of the Beretta. But the stairway was as silent as it was dark. When he was sure no one waited on the landing above, he started up, taking the steps two at a time. On the landing he felt for the wall with one hand.

He found himself wondering why Don Marshack would choose to live in a place like this. From what Marshack had said, his paintings did very well. According to Anna, he was a difficult man, and anything but popular among the gallery owners, but there was a market for his work, and he should have been able to afford something closer to human habitation.

The hall was long, but Bolan knew only one apartment occupied the entire fifth floor. Marshack liked the light, even claimed there was no better light in Paris. But at this time of night, all Bolan would see was the ambient light of the city.

He found the door with no trouble and pressed the
bell. He didn't hear a sound generated within—no
ring, no buzz, not even the moribund snarl of a
doorbell on its last legs. Dead silence greeted his
thumb the second time, as well.

Bolan rapped on the door, listening to the drum-
like echo of the metal-sheeted door rattle down the
hall. Still getting no answer, he tried the knob and
found the door open. It swung away from his hand,
then slammed into the wall with a dull thud that
came bouncing back at him from all sides. The studio was as black as a tomb, and the silence threat-
ened to swallow him whole.

"Marshack?" he called.

Something was wrong. Nobody covered a door
with sheet steel, then went out and left the door un-
locked. "Marshack?" When the Executioner got no
answer on the second call, he backed away from the
doorway and reached for the Beretta.

He raced down the hall to the landing, reached up
and smashed the naked light bulb with the barrel of
the Beretta. Then he turned and sprinted back the
way he'd come. He crossed the hall and groped along
the wall with his left hand, his arm crossed in front
of him.

His fingers finally found the molding of the door
frame, and he stopped. Listening intently, he held his
breath, trying to pick up the least sound that didn't
belong. What he heard was a distant car horn in the

street below. When that died out, the silence was total. Not even a hint of life from the other floors broke the stillness.

He thought about calling to Marshack one more time, but decided it was pointless. If anyone lay in wait in the studio, better to keep him guessing. Bolan got on the floor and crawled to the doorway, then wormed his way inside. The grit of the tiled hall gave way to the feel of smooth wood under his palms.

He moved to the right, wishing he had some idea of the layout. But he'd have to make do. As his eyes adjusted to the intense gloom, he could pick out shapes within a couple of feet, but they were so indistinct, he couldn't tell what they were. Still crawling, he hugged the wall for several feet without encountering an obstacle.

Sliding one hand up the wall, he felt the bottom edge of something, probably a canvas hanging on the wall. Raising himself up a little higher, he could feel the texture of the paint. The canvas gave under his fingers in an unnatural way. He got to his knees and let his hand wander across the painting, his fingers slipping through at one point. He could feel the ragged edge of the canvas, the thickly layered paint as sharp as a razor where it had been fractured.

Puzzled, he had the urge to stand and try to see what was wrong with the picture, but he couldn't allow himself to be distracted. He went down again and continued along the wall.

Ten feet farther, he bumped something with one hand. It echoed hollowly, and he thought he heard a sharp intake of breath.

Bolan froze where he was, then flattened himself against the floor. It was tempting to make a quick move, but he ran the risk of blundering into something or tripping. He reached tentatively for the object ahead of him. It was light, and sounded like metal.

Feeling along its side, the Executioner realized it was a can of some kind. At the top edge he felt the sharp lip, then some sticks. Paintbrushes. He took two of the brushes out of the can. Turning on his side, he flipped one across the room. It hit something soft, making a plopping sound, then clattered on the floor.

Immediately he heard that sharp intake of breath again, and this time he was certain. Someone else was in the studio. He tossed the second brush, and it clanged against metal. A single gunshot rang out, then a short burst. Maybe two men. He couldn't be sure.

The automatic weapon was suppressed, its muffled cough sending a hail of slugs across the room. But the first shot had sounded different, like a pistol. Bolan heard some glass break, But at least now he knew the presence was a lethal one.

It also hit him that Marshack was supposed to be here. He doubted the gunner was Marshack, but that meant the painter might be home at any minute, or already dead somewhere in the studio. There was no way to tell whether the gunner was after Bolan or Marshack—or if it mattered.

All the warrior knew was he had to do something and do it quickly. He reached for the can of brushes again and found three more. He flipped one in the same direction as the first two. It clanged off metal, then landed with another soft plop. Like the second, it provoked a burst of fire, but Bolan was still unable to get a fix on the sound. It was too furious and too abrupt to be pinpointed.

He had a flashlight, but using it was out of the question. Without cover he would be opening himself to instant death.

Bolan waited, hoping for a break, but there wasn't enough time. He took the next brush and thought about throwing it in the general direction of the gunshots, but he could be off by fifteen or twenty feet. He also knew that he might accidentally draw blind fire his way.

This time he threw two brushes, sending them in slightly different directions, as close as he could gauge to the corner of the studio. More gunfire erupted, then he got the break he was looking for.

The automatic weapon was empty. A sharp click signaled the removal of an ammo clip, and another the insertion of a fresh load. A single shot, again slightly different in sound, cracked from somewhere in the same vicinity. Two guns, and almost certainly two gunmen.

Bolan stretched toward the sound, trying to pin it down like an entomologist chasing an elusive bug avoiding the collector's pins. He squeezed off one shot, but it went wide, and shattered more glass. It sounded like it might be a window. They had to be covered with heavy draperies, Bolan thought. If he could get to them, he could rip them aside and let in some light.

The only other option, one that looked increasingly like it might be his only choice, was to try to get back out the door. At least that way he could intercept Marshack and prevent him from walking into the gunmen's line of fire. He was reluctant to do it, because he didn't know the layout of the studio. There might be another exit, and if the gunmen went out the other way, he'd never know who they were.

Bolan was getting impatient. He fired again, but came up empty, as near as he could tell. He leaned forward, trying to make out some movement in the darkness, anything to give him a target, but the uniform blackness looked like a single seam of coal.

The Executioner backed up to the wall again, found the can and picked it up. If there were brushes, maybe there was something he could use, a solvent, benzene . . . He took a sniff, and the sharp tang of mineral spirits hit him. He moved along the wall again, bringing the can with him. He wasn't sure how long the studio was, but wanted to get to the side wall away from the door.

The can cracked against something hard, and he flattened. A spray of lead ripped along the wall just inches above him. Bolan fired back two quick shots. Something scraped on the floor, and he knew he'd come close. The gunmen were getting nervous. He fired again, trying to home in on the whisper of sound, but it seemed to come from everywhere and nowhere at the same time.

He heard a click, and a shaft of gray light suddenly speared into the blackness. Bolan brought up the Beretta, ready to fire at the first hint of motion. A dull boom filled the huge room, and a shadow darted into the gray light and out again.

Suddenly the window was shattered by a barrage of gunfire.

Bolan hugged the floor until the shooting stopped, then pushed to his feet and ran toward the yawning window frame. He looked out on a catwalk that ran the length of the roof and saw a head drop down out of sight between iron guardrails.

The fire escape. Bolan raced toward the door the gunman had opened, nearly tripping over a prostrate form in one corner. He thought for a second it might be Don Marshack, but a quick glance told him otherwise. One of his shots had found a home. He ducked through the door and into a small chamber. Another door yawned open on the Parisian night. He ran through it, then raced along the outside of the window. At the top of the fire escape he ducked his head out and jerked it back. A short burst ripped up the ladder, making the iron rungs clang and generating a shower of sparks and paint chips that flew toward his face.

Bolan moved away from the ladder a few yards and peered over the edge. He could see the gunman racing along another catwalk two floors below. The warrior leaned out over the railing and fired once as the gunman flattened against the wall, then darted ahead and disappeared through another metal door.

The Executioner raced back to the studio exit and burst through the door and into the room just as it was flooded with light.

Don Marshack was standing in the doorway, his hand on a chain dangling from the ceiling. "What is this . . . ?"

"You had visitors."

9

Marshack looked at the dead man on the floor. In the harsh light from the bank of overhead fluorescent lights, the body looked small and doll-like. The corpse's beard seemed almost like an afterthought, like a clown's whiskers, pasted on but slightly askew.

"Have you ever seen him around the café?"

"I don't think so." He went through the man's pockets, not expecting to find anything. He didn't. Straightening, he looked around the studio, and his face seemed to dissolve. Bolan was thrown for a moment, then followed Marshack's gaze.

Painting after painting, those framed and hanging on the wall, several lined up along one wall in various stages of completion and two on large easels all had been slashed. A dozen or more slices through paint and canvas had turned them into ragged-edged vertical blinds.

"God Almighty!" Marshack screamed. "Look what they've done!" He turned to Bolan with a look of uncomprehending helplessness. "Look what they've done to my work!"

Bolan was at a loss. "I'm sorry, Marshack."

"Bastards." The painter turned his back and walked to the shattered window and braced his arms on the sill. Ignoring the slivers of glass that littered the narrow shelf, he leaned forward with his weight on the heels of his hands. Bolan heard him mumbling something under his breath. Marshack straightened, then, and walked to the rear door and out onto the walkway on the far side of the window bank.

The warrior joined him outside. The lowering sky had begun to give up its burden, and a fine mistlike drizzle drifted past the men, coating everything with a thin sheen of icy water.

"I really am sorry, Marshack."

"Sorry? You don't understand. Those canvases represent months of work, *months*. I've been working on some of them for two goddamned years. Do you understand what that means? Some of the others are six, seven years old. I don't paint like that anymore. I can't replace them. Ever."

"They must have known that."

Marshack nodded mutely.

"Are you sure you don't recognize that man in there?"

The Armenian shook his head. "Never seen him in my life. What about the other one? Did you get a look at him? Would you recognize him if you saw him again?''

"No. Not a chance."

"Why were they here? How did they know?"

"I think you have a better chance of answering that question than I do. Did you find anything tonight?"

"No. Nothing."

"I had better luck."

Marshack turned to look at him for the first time. Bolan studied his face. The collecting mist had already soaked the man's hair. It trickled down through his beard, glistened on his eyebrows, picking up the harsh light from inside the studio and vibrating as Marshack's agitated breathing made his whole body shiver.

"So," Marshack said, "tell me."

"I found Walter Jason and his wife."

"Where?"

"Right where Anna said they would be."

"But I don't understand. How could..."

"I don't know." Bolan took a deep breath. He looked out at the lights of the city. Across the Seine, a narrow band of moving lights from the nighttime traffic struggled with the mist. At that distance it looked more like disembodied globes of light following along in pairs. "Do you trust her?"

"I'm in love with her," Marshack said. It was so simple, it answered all questions, at least for Marshack.

But not for Bolan. "But do you *trust* her, Marshack?"

"I've known her for six years. She's never lied to me, never even misled me, as far as I know, not even unintentionally. Does that answer your question?"

"Yeah, I guess it does."

"But you're not satisfied, are you?"

Bolan turned and looked into the studio. Marshack followed his gaze. "Look at that," the warrior said. "There has to be some reason for that."

"You think she sent those men here? Is that what you're telling me?"

"It's possible. She gave us the addresses. She knew you'd be out. She knew we'd be meeting here. Those men didn't come here just to carve up your paintings. They wanted to kill somebody. You. Me. Both of us, probably."

"I know that. But there has to be some other explanation."

"What is it?"

"I don't know."

"Then we better ask her."

"No. We can't do that."

"If she didn't do it, she'll understand. And if she doesn't understand, then maybe she's not what you think she is."

"It's not that simple."

"It never is," Bolan replied. "Unless you make it that simple."

Marshack turned away to look at the city again. It was as if he couldn't bear to see the ruined canvases, as if it were too painful a sight.

Bolan gave it a little time to sink in. He could sense that Marshack was wrestling with a decision, one his head told him had to go one way and his heart another. The agent's old instincts were still there under the transformed veneer. The painter moved past him and walked back inside. He walked to the wall and stopped in front of the largest canvas, a nighttime cityscape rendered in blocks of dark pigments, the few lights like blind eyes staring back at him. He reached out with his right hand, let his fingers wander over the thickly layered paint then tracing one of the cuts from the bottom of the frame as high as he could reach.

He moved from one painting to another, sometimes moving quickly to the next, sometimes lingering, as if some of them meant more to him, and their destruction were more painful. When he'd completed his inventory of the devastation, he turned and looked through the broken glass. He nodded.

Bolan walked back to the door and stepped inside, shaking off the worst of the weather. Marshack had started to take the damaged paintings from the easels and placed them against the wall in a stack with the others. He moved around the studio until every canvas on the floor was in a single stack.

When he was finished, he looked at Bolan again. "All right."

"Here or at the café?"

"Here. I'll go get her."

"I'll go with you."

Marshack took one more look at the paintings on the wall, shook his head and said, "All right." He walked to the door, pulled the chain and plunged the studio back into darkness. Bolan glanced over his shoulder at the floating halos of the city beyond the shattered window, then followed Marshack to the door.

The Armenian led the way down the darkened stairwell. Something didn't seem right to Bolan, and he grabbed Marshack by the shoulder at the fourth-floor landing and pulled him back.

"Where's the light?" he whispered. "They were on when I got here."

"Me, too," the painter replied. "Maybe the second man hung around."

Bolan didn't belabor the obvious. "Is there another way out of here?"

"The same way he got out. Down the fire escape."

"Let's go." Bolan turned and led the way up the stairs, stopping in front of Marshack's door.

"Let's split up. If he's waiting there with the lights out, he's in the building. Maybe we can capture him and squeeze some intel."

"Good idea. I'll take the stairs."

"All right. I'll slam the door downstairs when I get there. As soon as you hear it, start down. I'll come up from below."

"You got it." Marshack opened the studio door to let Bolan in. "Be careful," he whispered.

"You too."

Marshack closed the door and locked it, trying to make as little noise as possible.

Bolan picked his way across the studio, then moved quickly along the windows until he reached the fire escape. He checked his weapons, took the safety off each, then started down. Two minutes later the Executioner was on the ground. He had to climb over an iron gate to get into the alley alongside the building, then went up the front stairs.

The street behind him was dark, and he didn't have to worry about being backlighted, but caution was second nature. The warrior flattened against the hallway wall, opened the inner door, slipped inside and let the door slam.

He listened to the hollow boom echo up and down the stairwell and knew that Marshack would have been able to hear it. Trying to figure out where the gunman went to ground wasn't easy. Probably not on the first floor, the warrior guessed. The gunman would have wanted some time, and to have his targets trapped on the stairs, so he would be somewhere between the second and fourth floors.

Staying flat against the wall, Bolan picked his way carefully up the stairs to the second-floor landing. He stopped every few moments to listen, but he heard nothing.

When the warrior was halfway up the next flight, a single shot rang out, then footsteps pounded on the steps. Bolan continued up to the next landing, where he crouched in the corner to cut down on his exposure. He heard another gunshot, and this time he saw the muzzle-flash. The man holding the weapon turned and raced toward him.

"Don't move!" Bolan shouted.

But the gunner kept coming, firing his suppressed Uzi on the run. Plaster gouged from the wall cascaded over the Executioner's shoulders as he squeezed the trigger. He heard the impact of the bullet on something resilient, then the clatter of a heavy object bouncing down the stairs.

"Belasko, are you all right?" Marshack shouted.

"Got him."

Bolan reached into his pocket for a small flashlight. He could hear Marshack on the stairs above as the light clicked on.

"Recognize him?" Bolan asked as the Armenian joined him.

"No." He pointed his pistol at the man lying on his back on the landing. "Bastard ruined years of work. For no damned reason." His hand quivered, and Bolan thought for a moment he was going to pull the trigger. But the painter finally let the gun drop to his side and turned away.

"Let's get the hell out of here," Marshack whispered.

10

Anna Chirkizian lived on a quiet street of middle-class two- and three-story garden apartment houses in the eastern suburbs. It was nearly two o'clock when Bolan parked the car in the small lot beside the building.

"That's odd," Marshack commented as they got out of the car.

"What?"

"There's a light on in Anna's apartment. Ordinarily she's asleep long before this."

"This hasn't been an ordinary day."

Marshack grunted. He stood on the pavement, looking up at the window. A heavy drapery obscured most of it, but a narrow band of light across the top and two thin filaments of light along either edge of the picture window left no doubt that a light was on.

"Maybe she fell asleep, or maybe she went out and left it on so someone would think she was home."

Marshack wasn't convinced. "No, that's not like her. If the light's on, she's there. She's predictable that way."

"Good to know you know so much about her."

"What's that supposed to mean?" Marshack said, closing the car door with a jerk of his wrist.

"If she's holding something back, if she's lying, you'll have a better chance of seeing it than I will."

Marshack shook his head. "No. She isn't lying. I'm sure of that."

"Why, because she sent you out in the cold with an address in your hand? Maybe she just wanted to keep you out of trouble while her friends took care of the *real* trouble."

"You mean you?"

"Think about it for a minute," Bolan said. "She gives you two addresses. She knows we'll split up, and she knows where we both are. If you're not there, you don't get hurt."

"You're accusing her of planning cold-blooded murder."

"Yes, I am."

"I don't believe it."

Bolan knew he wouldn't, but he wanted Marshack angry. He wanted him alert, questioning, suspicious. He would pay attention to every nuance, every hidden meaning, anxious to find the proof he believed was there. But he would notice things that he might otherwise have missed. As long as Marshack was paying attention, there just might be something to gain from the approaching confrontation. And Bolan was determined that it be confrontational. Too much was at stake to worry about bruised feelings.

Marshack started toward the front door of the building, not waiting for Bolan. He was angry, and he showed it by stomping down the pavement and ripping the lobby door back too far for its hinges. The door creaked, protested and swung back, slamming into Marshack's shoulder.

The Armenian had a key to the inner door and used it. He led the way down a dimly lighted hall to an elevator bank, stabbed the call button, then turned his back to it. He rocked up and down on his heels, his arms folded behind his back.

When the elevator arrived, he spun around before the door had a chance to open and stepped inside, holding the door until Bolan joined him. They made the ride in silence, Marshack picking at the edge of the polished plate holding the control bank, the Executioner watching him without comment.

The door opened with a rumble. A carpeted hall stretched away in both directions. Marshack went to the left, expecting Bolan to follow. As they drew close to the last door on the right-hand side, Marshack stopped. He'd heard something. Bolan heard it, too.

The warrior yanked his Beretta out of shoulder leather as Marshack drew. The door opened, and a man darted into the hall. He was already running by the time he spotted the two men blocking the corridor. He reached into his coat, but Bolan was too quick for him. He launched himself through the air and caught the smaller man with a shoulder just below the breastbone, sending him sprawling to the floor.

Bolan pinned the guy, and Marshack reached into the coat and found an H&K .32 automatic, the safety off. The Armenian straightened, and the warrior hauled the man to his feet.

Marshack headed toward Anna's apartment, the key in one hand and his pistol in the other.

The door swung open easily. "Anna? Anna?"

Bolan dragged the man toward the doorway and shoved him across the threshold without letting go of his coat. Marshack was already heading toward a door across a long, narrow living room.

Anna appeared in the doorway, a look of surprise mixed with fright on her face. "Don, what's wrong? What are you doing here?"

"We have to talk."

She saw Bolan then, and the captive still squirming like a fish on a gaff at the end of Bolan's outstretched left arm. "Aram? What—"

"Who is he?" Marshack asked.

"You know Aram. He comes to the café, works there sometimes. Aram Martoon." She glared at Bolan. "Let him go."

The warrior shook his head. "Not until we get some answers."

"What answers? Would somebody please tell me what's going on?"

Marshack, instead of answering, grabbed Martoon by the shoulder. He hauled him away from Bolan, yanked a closet open and shoved him in. He closed the door and twisted the thumb lock. Leaning close to the door, he said, "If I hear a peep out of you, I'll put six holes in the door. You understand?" When he got no answer, he smiled grimly and moved back toward the living room. "Come on."

Bolan and Anna followed him out of the small hallway. Marshack dropped into an easy chair. His damp coat squeaked on the soft leather of the chair as he adjusted his weight. Anna started toward him, but he shook his head. "Sit over there." He pointed with Aram's pistol. She saw the gun for the first time.

"What are you doing with that gun?"

"Trying to stay alive."

"What are you talking about, Don? Please, tell me what's going on...."

Marshack nodded at Bolan. "You tell her. I'm tired."

Anna turned to him then, lowering herself to the front edge of the sofa.

"We followed your leads, tonight," he said.

"Did you find anyone? Any of the hostages?"

"I did. Marshack didn't."

"And..." She leaned forward, trying to prompt him to continue. "Go on. I don't see the problem."

"The problem," Bolan said, "is what happened next. I was supposed to meet Marshack at his studio. I got there a little early. But I wasn't early enough. Somebody was already inside, waiting for one of us. Or both."

"Who was waiting?"

"We don't know. But they were there to kill somebody. Only it didn't work out that way." Bolan was watching her face closely. If she was surprised by what had happened, he didn't see any sign of it. But if she was disappointed that a carefully drawn plan had gone haywire, there was no sign of that, either. Her face was as rigid as a stone mask.

"They got away, then?"

Bolan shook his head. "No. They didn't get away."

"Oh."

Was that relief? Bolan wondered. "But while they waited, they killed time by slashing Marshack's paintings. All of them."

One hand went to her mouth then. Genuine surprise, Bolan was sure. Her eyes were focused somewhere above and behind him now, and he turned instinctively. She was staring at one of Marshack's paintings.

When he turned back, she was looking at Marshack and shaking her head. "Oh, Don," she said. "Oh, my God, that's..."

Bolan stared at her without expression. She sensed his hostility, but she wouldn't give him the satisfaction of asking. So he said, "I don't suppose you'd know anything about what happened tonight, then?"

"No."

"How did you know I would find two of the hostages at the Armenian school?"

"I have sources."

"What else do you have, Anna?"

"What do you mean?"

"I mean how much input do you really have into what's happened? You seem to know a great deal more than you've told me or Marshack."

"I—"

"Think about it very carefully, Anna. I don't think you realize just how serious this is. We are not talking about children's games here. We are talking about life and death. Innocent lives and very violent death. Have you ever seen what a bullet does to a man, Anna?"

She stiffened at that. Her eyes clouded over, as if she were trying not to see something that was all too clear in her memory. "I have seen that, yes."

"Anna," Marshack said, "Belasko is right. If you think you can just wade in the sewer and climb onto the curb anytime you want, you're wrong. Once you're in, you're in up to your neck, like it or not. And so am I. They know I'm involved now, and I can't get out until it's finished."

"My father," she whispered.

"What about him?" Marshack walked over to kneel beside her.

"They killed him. They shot him in the back of the head while I watched. They *forced* me to watch."

"Who, Anna?" Bolan coaxed.

"Hampirian's people. Those animals in the APS. I had to watch, damn it."

"Anna, what do you know? What are you holding back?" Bolan asked gently.

"I know that I don't know everything." She raised her face to look at Marshack. "I didn't mean for any of this to happen. Martell wanted me to help. I thought I could get even. But now..." Her voice trailed off. "Now I don't know."

"Do you know where all the hostages are, Anna? We are talking about seven innocent people. You have to realize that."

"Six," she whispered. "Just six..."

"But there were seven people kidnapped."

"They killed the chauffeur. Martell sent word. They made a video tape of the murder and sent it to Radiguet."

She got up and walked to the window. Opening the draperies, she cranked open one of the casement windows. The cool air made Bolan realize how oppressive it was in the room.

"Let Aram tell you," Anna said. "He saw the tape. I just . . ." She turned away.

Marshack walked to the closet and opened the door. Martoon was cowering in the corner. Marshack had to reach in and grab him by the coat to get him out.

Bolan looked at him. "Tell us about the tape, Aram."

Martoon started to shake. Anna got up from the sofa and went to him. She cupped his chin in her hands. "Tell them, Aram. It's all right. Just tell them."

The young man nodded, as Anna's hands fell away. "It was terrible," he said. "They—"

The sudden explosion of blood and brain tissue stunned them.

"The light," Bolan shouted. "Get the light." He dragged Anna to the floor as Marshack knocked over the lamp.

Aram didn't notice.

11

Savoog Hampirian sat on a stool, shaking his head. Norman Charlton was shouting, but Hampirian seemed not to notice. When the American finally stopped to catch his breath, Hampirian nodded. "You should take it easy, Mr. Charlton. Your face is red. You are shaking. Do you have trouble with high blood pressure, perhaps?"

"What are you, some kind of comedian? You must be insane. Why shouldn't I shout? What the hell is wrong with you?"

"There is nothing wrong with me, Mr. Charlton. I can assure you of that. I just want to make certain that you are not ill. That would not be good for either of us. It would complicate this entire affair enormously. Neither of us wants that."

"I don't give a damn whether your life is complicated or not. I want to get the hell out of here. Now!"

"That is not possible, I am afraid. We have taken a step that is irreversible. Before we can turn you loose, certain conditions must be met."

"What do you want, money? I can get you money. I can get you as much money as you want."

"Money is as nothing, Mr. Charlton. What we want, you cannot give us."

"Then why are we here? Why are you holding us?"

"I don't think you would understand."

"Try me."

"Some other time, perhaps. For the moment I just want to inform you that there have been no new developments, and that is very distressing to us. If nothing happens in the next twenty-four hours, then it might be necessary to take a further step."

"What are you talking about? What kind of step?"

"I haven't decided on that yet. But I will have to very soon. If there is anything you need in the way of medication, please tell me now. I will not be back for a day or maybe two. I am not interested in causing you any harm. You are of no value to us unless you are alive and well. I want to do everything in my power to make certain you stay that way."

"Then let us go."

"That is one thing I cannot do. Not now. If our request is honored, then..." Hampirian turned his palms up. "But there is no point in discussing that now."

Hampirian got to his feet. Charlton tried to break out of the chair, but his hands were cuffed tightly behind him, and his ankles were tied to the chair legs. There was nothing he could do, and the impotence made him all the more furious. He started to rage again, and Hampirian nodded. The man standing behind the Armenian leaned forward and whipped a thick cloth around the man's face, brought it up over his mouth and knotted it securely.

Hampirian walked to the door, then turned. "Please try to cooperate, Mr. Charlton. It is best for both of us." He clicked off the light and closed the door.

The guard followed him across the cellar and up the stairs. When they were on the main floor, Hampirian shut off the light and closed the cellar door. "Check on them every couple of hours, Michael. If there is a problem, you know where to reach me."

"He is no trouble, Professor," the guard. "He makes a lot of noise, but other than that, nothing we can't handle."

"The woman?"

"She is taking it better than he is."

"The women always do. I think they are braver than we are, Michael, stronger. I suppose they have no choice."

The guard laughed. Hampirian walked to the back door and stepped outside. The guard followed him onto the porch and waited while he walked to his car. When the headlights came on, Ekizian went back inside. His shift was almost over, and he was tired. He went to the small kitchen and poured himself a cup of coffee. With an hour left, he was going to have to struggle to keep awake.

The farmhouse was nearly a hundred miles southeast of Paris, and Hampirian had a long drive. Ekizian didn't envy him, but at the moment he'd rather be just about anyplace other than where he was. Baby-sitting two cranky Americans was no picnic.

He sipped the coffee, letting the heat soak into his bones. He set the cup down, then listened. It sounded like someone had knocked on the back door. He wondered whether Hampirian had forgotten something. When the noise wasn't repeated, he picked up the cup, downed the rest of the coffee and walked to the basement door.

He didn't like staying in the basement. It was damp and chilly in the outer room, and it was drafty. He could hear tiny feet skittering around in the beams overhead, and he hoped they belonged to mice. Descending the stairs, he kept one hand on the wooden railing, the other on the butt of a pistol stuck in his belt.

At the bottom of the steps he heard another thump, but it was distant, as if it had come from the second floor. Maybe one of those lazy bastards was waking up early for a change, he thought. Another thump stopped him in his tracks. It was a heavy sound, one that shook the old house, and he knew something was wrong.

Pulling the gun he turned and started back up the stairs. He slipped the safety off and stopped just inside the doorway, one foot on the landing and one on the last step.

Tentatively he stuck his head through the doorway. "Vartan?" he called. "Emile?" Neither man answered him. He was starting to sweat now, despite the chill. The gun felt heavy in his hand, and his palms were making the gun butt slippery.

"Vartan?"

He heard footsteps, but no one answered him. He told himself that Hampirian had forgotten something and come back for it. But he hadn't heard the car, and he hadn't heard the door, which was locked from inside in any case.

He moved toward the stairs leading to the second floor. Turning into the cramped hallway, he stopped to look up the steep flight of steps. The second floor was dark. There still had been no repeat of the heavy thumping, and the footsteps, if that's what they were, had stopped.

Once more, he called, "Vartan? Emile?" He didn't want to go upstairs. What he wanted more than anything was to go down to the basement and lock the door behind him. But if something was wrong and he did nothing, Hampirian would have his head.

So he took one step toward the stairwell. He saw boots now, on the second-floor landing, barely visible in the wash of light from the kitchen. Something was definitely wrong. He started to back away from the stairs at the same time the boots moved toward the top step.

He bumped into a chair and lost his balance. He stumbled and reached out with his right hand to grab on to the door frame. Knocking his gun against the wooden molding, he lost his grip on it and it rattled into the kitchen. He tried to keep his balance, but he couldn't and toppled to the floor. Turning onto his knees, he crawled after the pistol, feeling faintly silly. But something told him he needed the gun.

His fingers closed over the butt, and he turned as the boots came into view just outside the door. As he was bringing the gun up, he accidentally squeezed the trigger, and the report of the heavy automatic scared him.

Whoever was outside the doorway backed up. And in his desperation, Ekizian squeezed the trigger again and again, sending a barrage of 9 mm slugs through the plasterboard wall to the right of the door frame. When the man collapsed to the floor across the doorway, Ekizian started to shake. He looked at the body, the smears of blood on the dark shirt, and the staring eyes for a long moment, then let out a low moan that seemed as if it would never stop.

He moved toward the dead man, stopping in the doorway. He would have to step across the body, but was afraid. He had to go upstairs, to see why Vartan hadn't answered him.

At the top of the stairs, he stopped to catch his breath. He could hear his heart hammering away, feel it thumping against his rib cage. He went toward one of the bedrooms, guiding himself with his left hand flat on the wall. His right hand still held the pistol. He tried to remember how many times he had fired, but couldn't count the shots.

At the doorway, he stopped. He listened, hoping to hear Vartan's raspy snore, but the room was perfectly silent. He stepped through the doorway and clicked on the light. Vartan lay half on the floor, a blood-soaked sheet tangled around his legs holding him to the bed. Ekizian shook his head. He wanted to scream, but knew that no one would hear him. He turned then and ran to the second bedroom. This time, he clicked the light on right away.

Emile lay in the bed, staring at the ceiling. The blue blanket had turned dark red over his chest. Ekizian moved closer, not knowing why. He reached down to close the sightless eyes, then turned back toward the door. This time he did scream, knowing it was pointless and not caring. He had something inside him that had to get out, terror, rage, he wasn't sure, but was conscious of trying to give it a name as it scorched his throat and lungs.

He saw the man in the doorway then. The man looked familiar, but Ekizian didn't know why. He raised the gun, but couldn't get it all the way up. It was too heavy. He saw the ugly submachine gun, the thick black cylinder screwed to the muzzle, and he knew then why he hadn't heard the gunshots, or rather why they had sounded like distant thumps on the floor.

He looked at the man with the gun and closed his eyes. He heard the first lethal spit of the Uzi, felt something tear through his chest before he started to fall.

The gunman fired again, a short burst, just to be sure. He turned then and walked down the stairs. Three men met him at the bottom of the stairwell. "Get rid of the bodies," he said. "I'll find the Americans."

He went down to the basement. He knew right where to look. When he opened the door, he saw Norman Charlton struggling with the ropes that bound him, his arms still cuffed behind the chair back. Charlton saw the gun and his eyes widened in alarm.

The man walked toward Charlton and pulled a heavy knife, serrated on one edge, and knelt beside the chair. He bent, cut the ropes, then grabbed Charlton by the shoulder and hauled him to his feet.

He left the gag in place and dragged the limping American back to the main room of the basement.

"Wait here," he said, then moved away, off to a dark corner of the cellar. Charlton saw a wash of light then as a door opened. A moment later he saw Lois, her hands cuffed behind her back. She stumbled through the doorway and ran toward him. The man with the gun stood at the bottom of the stairs, and gestured with his weapon. "Up."

12

Marshack crawled across the floor to Anna. He stroked her hair, trying to calm her. "Anna, listen to me. You must tell us everything. You must. Whatever you know might save our lives, as well as those of the hostages. Do you understand?"

With his fingers tangled in her long black hair, he felt her head bob up and down. To Bolan he said, "I'll take Anna into the bedroom away from the window."

"I'll go outside and see what I can find."

"Be careful."

The Executioner waited until he heard the bedroom door close before he crawled to the window. To the left of the single large pane of glass, he saw the bullet hole, just a foot or so above the sill. Sighting back he would be able to see where the bullet struck Aram and the wall behind him, but in the dark, he had to do it by memory.

Moving to the edge of the window, he stood and peered around the window frame into the street below. The shot had been fired from street level or just a little above, perhaps from the roof of a car.

Nothing seemed out of the ordinary. He made his way out to the hallway, and headed for the fire stairs, which were located at the rear of the building. He opened the heavy fire door and sprinted down the stairs, taking them two at a time. He went out the back way and along the rear of the building until he found a broad strip of lawn that gave him access to the street.

At the corner of the building, only partly covered by a clump of sculpted yews, he watched the opposite side of the street for several minutes. When he was satisfied no one lurked in the shadows, he sprinted to the other side. Standing at the corner of a building almost identical to Anna's, he looked up at her apartment.

A streetlight clearly showed the bullet hole. The ragged edge of the hole and the irregular lace of cracks radiating out from it picked up the light and glittered like a silver web on the dark glass.

Convinced that the assassin was gone, he scoured the area for evidence of the shooting. The grass was too wet to show signs of footsteps, and the only bare earth was in the flower beds along the wall of the building. A quick survey turned up nothing. Bolan moved to the gutter where he found a heel print at the edge of the curb. By itself, it meant nothing, but when he looked more closely, he saw something shiny in the clear water running along the curb. A shell casing.

He bent to retrieve it and walked over to the streetlight to examine his find—a 7.62 mm NATO round. But he couldn't identify the weapon from the shell, since it was a common load.

Crossing the street, he went into the vestibule and pressed the bell for Anna's apartment. Expecting to hear the buzz of the intercom, he waited patiently for thirty seconds, then stabbed the button again. No answer. He was about to press the button again when he saw Marshack sprinting toward him.

The painter opened the door and stepped out into the vestibule. "I've got another address," he said. "Anna swears it's the only other one she knows about. If it is the only one, we should find the remaining hostages."

"And if not?" Bolan asked.

Marshack shrugged. "I don't know."

"Do you believe her?"

"Yes. She's scared out of her wits. I think something's gone very wrong, and she doesn't know why or how."

"What's she going to do?"

"She insists on staying here. She says she'll make some calls, see if she can learn anything. Some people owe her favors. She'll try to collect."

"If that shot was intended for her, they might think they got her. But if she contacts anyone, they'll know she's not dead."

"I told her that, but she says she'll move after she makes the calls. She can go to her uncle's place, near Bracieux. She thinks she'll be safe there."

"Do you?"

"I don't know."

"Why don't you go with her? I'll meet you there as soon as I can."

"You might need help. I can't let you walk into a minefield alone."

"I've done it before."

Marshack stared at him for a few seconds. "I believe you have. All right. Let me give you the addresses." He pulled a pad and ballpoint out of his coat pocket and wrote them down. Tearing off the page, he handed it to Bolan. "Do you know how to get to these places?"

"I'll find them. You have a car?"

"We'll take Anna's. Look, Belasko, I trust Anna. I really do. But I think there's more going on than she knows. You watch your back. I'll find out what I can, and we'll take it from there."

Bolan nodded. He waited until Marshack went back inside, then ran to his rented car. It was raining harder now, heavy drops of water pounding on the roof of the Peugeot as he started it up. The address

Marshack had give him was a freight warehouse down by the Seine, in the commercial district.

It took him thirty minutes, and he spent the time sorting through what had happened. It seemed that events were picking up speed. Something was giving them momentum, but he didn't know what or why. The murder of the chauffeur wasn't just an escalation. It was meant as a warning that other hostages would be sacrificed. Like terrorists the world over, whoever was in charge wanted everyone to know he meant business. That wasn't surprising, but it did seem like an abrupt leap forward, as if someone had a short fuse.

And he realized that Martell's injunction on contacting him no longer had any meaning. It had been meant to protect Bolan, to protect Anna and to protect the hostages. But it hadn't helped the chauffeur. He had to talk to Martell, and he hoped he could convince Anna Chirkizian to go with him. She seemed confused as well as frightened, and she just might agree, if he pushed her hard enough, and if he could convince Marshack to lend a hand.

But first things came first. And first he had to find the hostages. There was one other change in the ground rules. Now it made no sense just to find the hostages. If he got lucky and managed to locate some or all of them, he was determined to get them out. Saving two lives was better than losing seven. He didn't much like the mathematics, but it wasn't his choice.

He found the warehouse without difficulty. It was one of six in a row. Behind them, a railroad ran along the river. A series of bridges crossed the rail yards to give access to barges, small ships and their cargoes. Paris wasn't really a seaport, but freight haulers could negotiate the river. He pulled the car off the road, tucked it in an alley and jogged to the rail yard. A high cyclone fence separated it from the river and ran under the bridges to the pier side. But if he could get over the fence, he could use one of the ramps leading up to the back of the warehouses.

The fence was eight feet high, but had no barbed or razor wire on top. He leaped up, grabbed the steel pipe supporting the screen in both gloved hands and hauled himself to the top. Careful not to catch himself on the rusted ends of the wire, he tossed one leg over and lifted his torso off the pipe, letting the momentum of one leg carry the other over. He dropped to the gravel and sprinted toward a retaining wall made of railroad ties that towered above him. He could smell the creosote soaking the ties as he moved along the barrier to the first ramp. Glancing up, he saw a gate at the top of the ramp, but it was open. He climbed onto the ramp halfway up and sprinted toward the freight yard behind the warehouses.

A weathered sign hanging over the second warehouse from the left read Artemian's Orientalia, Importers to the Trade. That was his target. He watched the rear of the building for several minutes, trying to piece together the layout. He had seen the front only briefly as he drove past. It sported half a dozen large corrugated doors, the kind that rolled up.

The rear of the building had four more of the doors, each located between a pair of concrete piers jutting out into the freight yard. Dirty glass in an unbroken row of casement windows ran across the main freight dock across the back. Above the dock, but below the windows, a broad roof slanted down away from the building to cover the dock.

Bolan knew better than to hope the doors were open. They would make far too much noise in any case. From his position, he couldn't tell whether the windows could be opened. That might be his only way in, unless there was some kind of entrance on either side wall.

Bolan was about to sprint toward the left to check out that side of the warehouse, when he saw something moving in the shadows between two warehouses. He backed down the ramp a little, staying just below ground level, watching the spot. For a moment he thought his eyes had been playing tricks on him. But after nearly a minute, he saw movement again.

Someone raced across the space between the buildings and disappeared in the darkness against the wall. Two minutes later, another figure made the same dash.

One of the figures detached itself from the shadows and climbed onto the loading dock. Bolan started to crawl up the ramp to get a better look. He considered the possibility that it was French police, maybe a tactical squad. Maybe Martell had been mining another vein and struck pay dirt.

If they were police, and if he made a move, he might spoil the assault and get himself killed into the bargain. But what if they weren't police? It was a distinct possibility given what had happened at Marshack's studio, the murder of Aram and the gunplay at the apartment house in Rue Balzac.

It was beginning to look as if someone else was after the hostages. But who? And more to the point, why?

Bolan eased up the ramp. He could see the dim outline of one man scrambling onto the roof over the loading dock. He watched as a second man climbed onto the dock and made his way up to the roof.

A third man stepped out of the shadows and onto the dock, but made no attempt to gain the roof. Bolan dashed to a nearby tractor trailer, slipped down the far side, keeping the truck between him and the men until he reached the front tires of the cab.

The two men on the dock roof were spaced about thirty feet apart. Bolan raced across thirty feet of open ground until he reached the end of the dock. He stayed below the edge, out of the third man's line of sight.

He was halfway to the far end when he heard breaking glass. The lethal spit of silenced automatic rifles hissed high above him. The men on the roof were firing into the warehouse. Lights flashed on outside the building. The men on the roof weren't police. The warrior was certain of that.

Bolan climbed onto the dock. Sensing his presence, the man turned and opened up with a submachine gun. The Executioner dived to the dock and fired the Beretta.

The man staggered back and grasped at the edge of the door frame. He fell as Bolan scrambled to his feet. Two more men appeared around the corner just as a deafening explosion took out the door.

Bolan heard shouts from inside the building as the two new arrivals scrambled toward the door. The warrior nailed one with a second shot from the Beretta, but the second guy had retreated into the warehouse before Bolan could get a bead on him.

He heard the whine of a truck starter, then a roar as the engine caught. It was coming from the warehouse. Bolan raced to the doorway and hesitated before running inside. Across the wide open space he could see a big truck, its rear doors open. Two men were handing a woman up to another pair of men.

Bolan saw the two raiders hunkered down behind a mound of rugs rolled into tight cylinders.

One of them turned around. Sparks were flying behind the truck as the men on the dock roof continued to fire at it. Bolan turned then, picked one of the men out against the night sky and fired. He shifted to the .44 Desert Eagle, wanting more knockdown power. A second shot through the broken window erased the gunman. The second, more to the right, ducked away from the broken windows, and Bolan lost sight of him.

The truck was rolling now as the two men scrambled in and pulled the doors shut. One of the freight doors was up, and the truck barreled straight for it. The two gunmen raced after it. Bolan charged after them, conscious of the rifleman above and behind him, but unable to do anything about it at the moment.

The truck rolled through the door and squealed as it turned left. Bolan dropped to one knee and banged away with the .44 Magnum. One man reached for his back and fell forward, slamming into a pile of cardboard cartons. They must have been empty, because he took them out like a bowling ball in the pocket, and he was lost from view as the boxes cascaded over him. The second gunner raced through the door and into the street.

Bolan sprinted after him. He stopped for a split second at the doorway, then crouched and darted out of the building.

The gunman was gone. So was the truck.

And the hostages.

13

Bolan waited in the shadows at the end of the row of warehouses. He had told Martell to come alone, and to hurry. He wasn't sanguine about either possibility, and was determined to wait and see before exposing his position to the Frenchman. Twenty minutes later, a car rolled onto the street and drifted along the curb. It slowed further as it reached the front of Artemian Oriental Importers. The car stopped, backed up and turned into the warehouse.

In the warehouse lights, Bolan could see a solitary man at the wheel, but he was too distant to tell whether it was Martell. He started down the street, keeping close to the front of the buildings. He could just see the taillights of the six-year-old Renault, the kind of car Martell said he would be driving.

As Bolan reached the warehouse next to Artemian's, he heard a car door slam. He peered around the corner and saw Martell run into the warehouse, then stop and kneel beside one of the fallen gunmen.

Martell turned the body over on its back and shook his head.

"Know him?" Bolan asked as he crept up behind the Frenchman.

Martell leaped to his feet and reached for his gun, but stopped when he recognized the big American. He made a feeble pass at a smile. "No. I've never seen him before."

"Come on," Bolan said, "we have a long drive. I'll tell you everything on the way."

"Where are we going?"

"You'll see when we get there." He walked back to Martell's car and climbed into the driver's seat, adjusted the bucket to accommodate his longer legs and waited for Martell to get in the passenger side.

Martell opened the door. "I better call this in."

"You mean you didn't?"

"You said come quickly and tell no one. I took you at your word."

"All right, but hurry up." He watched Martell through the windshield as he walked to a phone mounted on a steel column twenty yards into the building. The man dialed, then turned his profile toward Bolan, as if to demonstrate that he had no secrets. He spoke rapidly, bobbing his head several times.

Martell hung up, ran back to the car, climbed in and slammed the door. "Let's get away from here quickly. I've never done that before in my life."

"Done what?"

"Left an anonymous tip. It's a strange feeling. I feel dirty, sort of."

"Why anonymous?"

"Something tells me there will be many questions. I certainly don't have the answers, and I don't want to have to respond to those questions until I'm ready."

"You're all right, Martell."

"I may soon be unemployed, as well."

The Executioner backed out of the garage and cruised down the block until he found his car. He pulled over and opened the door. "We'll drop your car off on the way. You won't want anyone to stumble on it down here, and I don't want mine turned up, either. I'll follow you."

Martell slid over the console into the driver's bucket as Bolan climbed out. Starting his own car, the warrior fell in behind the lieutenant on a half-hour drive to the suburbs. Martell lived in a high rise south of the city. Bolan waited at the curb while the Frenchman took his car into the underground garage, then walked back up the ramp. Once in the car, he said, "How did that business happen at the warehouse?"

Bolan pulled away from the curb. He was aware of Martell's eyes on him, and he was trying to decide just how much to tell. "Anna Chirkizian gave me some information. She claimed one or more of the hostages was being held there. I went to check it out."

"You weren't going to try to rescue them yourself, were you, before we've located them all?"

"They've already killed one man. The way I see it, the only way to protect the others is to extract them when and where we find them. But it's getting more complicated than that. And it didn't make any difference, because I never had a chance to decide."

"What do you mean?"

"I mean, someone else is tracking the hostages as well. That corpse in the warehouse belonged to one of them. I don't know who they are and Anna doesn't, either, or so she says."

"But that makes no sense."

"I'm not so sure. You said yourself émigré politics are Byzantine. Maybe you were more right than you knew. Anna told me her father had been killed by the APS. What I want to talk to her about is whether there's another group, maybe more than one. Rivals. That happens all the time. I'm sure you know that. The underdogs always fight among themselves. It seems to be a law of nature. My guess is that's what's going on here. But I don't know that for certain."

"But why would another group want to kidnap people from the original kidnappers?"

"I don't know. Maybe they want to buy credibility with the other émigrés. Maybe they want to turn them loose and earn gratitude from your government and mine. In exchange for something more than a friendly handshake, of course."

"Such as?"

"Guns. Money. It's neat, actually. The kidnappers demand favors. The second group earns them, at the expense of a rival group."

"You don't really believe that."

"I don't know what to believe. That's why I want to talk to Anna. Marshack is convinced that—"

"Who's Marshack?"

"Her boyfriend. You don't know him?"

Martell shook his head. "No. But it doesn't surprise me. Anna is very...private. Very discreet, almost paranoid in her insistence on secrecy."

"Yeah, well, it isn't working so well."

"What do you mean?"

"Somebody got wasted in her apartment tonight. I'm still not sure she wasn't the target. It was damn close, and it happened so fast it was hard to tell. You mean you don't know about that, either?"

"No, I don't. Who was killed?"

"A guy named Aram Martoon."

"What happened?"

"Sniper." Bolan reached into his pocket and found the shell casing. He flipped it to Martell. "That's all he left behind."

"Poor Aram."

"He never knew what hit him. He was one of yours, wasn't he?" Bolan said.

"Yes."

"Which means Anna might have had him hit, doesn't it?"

Martell didn't say anything. He didn't really have to.

Bolan turned off the main road to bypass Orleans. They still had about twenty miles to go. According to Anna, the farm was in an isolated stretch of country southeast of Blois in the lake country. Bolan didn't want to talk, and Martell seemed just as happy not to disturb the silence.

They picked up 922 at la Ferte-Saint Aubin, heading south, took the cutoff to Bracieux, due west of Neung. The road was dark and narrow, but in the absence of light, Bolan was able to relax. They would be able to see headlights half a mile ahead or behind. At Bracieux he passed through the sleepy village, found the turn and headed south.

They found the farm with no difficulty and turned into the long, winding lane between two rows of cypresses. As the car rolled to a stop in front of the house, Marshack came out to meet them.

"You all right?" he asked.

Bolan nodded.

Marshack looked at Martell. "Who are you?"

"That's Lieutenant Martell, DST."

"What the hell did you bring him here for?"

"He and Anna are old friends."

"What?"

"Let Anna explain," Bolan said. "Where is she?"

"Inside."

Marshack turned to lead the way in, but he kept glancing back over his shoulder at Martell. Anna was sitting at a broad table in the kitchen. Covered with a lace cloth, it seemed to take up half the room. An old coffeepot was on the stove, and three cups were already laid in their saucers.

When Anna saw Martell, she scowled, but didn't seem surprised. Instead of saying anything, she got up, walked to a cabinet and got an extra place setting.

"Anna, how are you?" Martell asked.

She didn't answer him. Making herself busy with coffee, cream and sugar, she filled the cups, placed a sugar bowl and creamer in the center of the table and sat down.

"All right," Bolan said, sitting at the table, "I want the whole truth, Anna, and I want it now. No lies."

"Wait a minute," Marshack snapped. "Don't talk to her like that."

"I'm right, and Anna knows it. Between her and Martell, here, there's got to be something we're just not focusing on. There's a piece missing, and I don't know whether it's by design or accident. But I'm going to find out, and I'm going to find out right now."

Anna took a sip of coffee. She put the cup down and stared into the dark liquid. Without looking up, she asked, "What do you want to know?"

"For starters, how did you know where the hostages were? And don't give me that garbage about sources."

"I . . . Someone who works with the APS is . . ."

"Anna, there's no time for this."

She nodded. "I know. I'm sorry." She stood and turned her back to the table. "I had an affair with Hampirian. He confided in me. He told me almost everything, and what he didn't tell me, I was able to figure out from his papers. He makes notes on everything, because he's so absentminded. He—"

"You slept with the man who had your father killed?"

"Yes. I'm not proud of it, but I did it, because I had to. I wanted to get even. I wanted the man who pulled the trigger, not just that fat bastard by himself. I had to get close to him somehow, and it was the best way." She shrugged, as if to suggest it was too obvious for explanation.

No one spoke for a long time. Anna couldn't bring herself to look at anyone. "But I don't know what's happening now. I swear to you, I don't. I haven't seen him in weeks."

"Do you know anyone who would want to undermine the APS from inside? Is there another group that has the manpower and the weapons to take on the APS?"

She nodded. "Yes. There is a paramilitary group called the Armenian Heritage. It is composed of former officers in the Red Army. They want control of Armenia. They are planning a civil war, as soon as they get enough weapons and money. The man who shot my father is a man named Haroun, Thomas Haroun. He is close to Hampirian, but he is a plant. He actually works for Armenian Heritage."

"Do you know who the others are?"

She shook her head. "Only rumors. That's all I know. Hampirian knows, but he never talks about them. Never mentions them by name. He is a dreamer, a clown. He thinks if you don't talk about them, they aren't real."

"Are you sure?"

She nodded. "There is one name, though. One I kept hearing. But only whispers. Vagueness, indirection. He was not high up, but..."

"Who is he?" Bolan demanded.

"Michael Ekizian."

"Christ," Martell exploded. "He's on my payroll!"

"Then I guess that explains a few things doesn't it?" Bolan said, looking at Martell. "I guess it's your turn to talk, Lieutenant."

14

Martell's directions to the safehouse were explicit. It was a long shot, and Bolan knew it. But they were almost out of options. It could just be coincidence that one of Martell's men was in Hampirian's inner circle, and also a member of Armenian Heritage. It could also be a coincidence that DST had a safehouse in the area of Bracieux, one that Ekizian was in a position to know about. The last place DST would look for the kidnapped Americans was on its own real estate.

Martell had gone back to Paris, determined to turn over every last rock. Bolan would check the safehouse, just to make sure, while the lieutenant trawled in more uncertain waters for a more elusive fish.

The farmhouse was dark when Bolan got there. He crouched behind a fieldstone wall a hundred yards from the rear. Beyond the house, a large barn and a low shed backed up against a stand of trees. The trees looked white in the faint moonlight, as if they were made of bone. The warrior settled down to watch the house for a while. There was no sign that the place was inhabited, but it appeared to be well maintained. The lawn had been trimmed toward the end of summer. Weeds grew on the inside of the wall, but stopped abruptly a few feet away from it.

Moving along the wall, Bolan worked his way to one corner, where it dwindled away to a few rocks piled haphazardly. A hedge joined it at right angles and ran in a straight line toward the barn. Staying in a crouch, he moved behind the chest-high hedge until he was directly opposite the house. He was looking at the two-story building, end-on now. A single window broke the smooth face of the house, on the second floor. It was just as dark as those in front.

The Executioner crept closer. The moonlight enabled him to spot a well-worn path that led to the barn. The traffic had left bare earth, a dull gray under the pale light.

It was beginning to look as if this lead was a dead end. He followed the hedgerow until he reached the barn. Behind the building a patch of damp earth glistened with a skin of water from yesterday's rain. The ground showed the deep tread of large tires, possibly a tractor, and dozens of footprints. The Executioner moved closer, dropping to one knee to examine the prints. Most were what he would have expected, boots with rippled gum soles, work boots. But several of the prints looked out of place—thin-soled shoes. He could see where the mud had oozed up and over the sole, the pattern of stitching tracing the outline of the soles, as if someone had worn new shoes in the mud, not exactly what a farmer would do.

Bolan looked up at the barn door. It was latched, a heavy padlock hooked through the hasp, but the lock was open. To the right of the door, a permanent ladder was nailed to the side of the building. The warrior glanced at the roof, nearly twenty-five feet above him. He tracked the prints of the new shoes then, half expecting them to go to the ladder, but they didn't. They marched in a straight line away from the barn, out into the field. Another row of prints from the same shoes ran straight to the barn door and disappeared behind it.

Bolan started up the ladder. At the roofline, a row of cleats ran up toward the peak. Easing himself over the edge, the warrior crept across the roof. He was conscious that someone might be inside the barn, so he tried to muffle his footsteps. From the ridge of the roof, he could see the house clearly. It was just as still and dark as when he arrived.

A trapdoor halfway along the front of the roof had been thrown back. The warrior lay prone and crawled toward the opening until he was no more than a foot away. He listened at the dark hole, but heard nothing, then leaned closer. The interior of the barn was coal black. He could see nothing through the square hatch. Groping inside with one hand, he found a ladder.

The open door troubled the warrior. It had rained for the past couple of days. Why would the hatch have been left open? He reached into his coat for a flashlight. Leaning close to the edge, he reached the light inside to keep it below the roof and clicked it on. He half expected a shout, but nothing happened. He peered into the barn's interior.

He was looking down on a loft. Bales of hay, some rope and old farm instruments, most rusty and cobwebbed, stood in one corner.

Beyond the lip of the loft, he could see a portion of the ground floor. The inside of the rear door was visible, as was a strip of hay-littered packed earth a few feet wide from corner to corner. The ground was soft and damp directly in front of the door, but Bolan was too far away to tell whether there were visible prints.

Clicking the light off, he tucked it back into his pocket and swung his legs over the opening. He found the first rung of the ladder easily and dropped into the loft. Once on the floor, he used the light again, looking down into the cavernous interior of the lower floor.

An old tractor sat in one corner, but there were no other vehicles. A harrow stood on end, its hitch high in the air, and a row of tools hung on a partition of raw wood. Hay littered the floor. He walked to the door and got down on his hands and knees to examine the damp earth. The shoe prints he'd seen outside were there, but disappeared on the dry ground away from the door.

He stood and walked to the partition, looked behind it, but found nothing. The front door of the barn, which slid on rollers to one side, was partway open. Through the opening, he could see the back of the house. He checked out the back door, then the blank windows on both floors. The curtains hung limply from the rods, betraying no evidence of anyone inside.

The Executioner unleathered his Beretta 93-R, set it for single shots and gave the house one more quick scan. When he saw nothing, he slipped through the opening, sprinted across the wide yard and crouched below a window to the left of the rear door. He listened intently for several minutes, but heard nothing.

When Bolan turned the knob gently, he discovered that it was locked. That was to be expected, and it made the place seem more normal, as if its inhabitants had gone away for the night. But he wanted to look inside, just to be sure. A safehouse was supposed to look normal, to be peaceful and unobtrusive. It was hard to imagine any place more perfectly tranquil than this one.

A second-floor window was located above the small porch roof. Rather than break the lock downstairs or break a window, he would try it, on the off chance it was open. It was essential that Ekizian not know that anyone was on to him. Bolan didn't want to tip his hand if it could be avoided, and if it couldn't be, well, he'd deal with it then.

Bracing one foot on a first-floor windowsill, he managed to get up onto the small roof. It felt as if it were swaying a little under his weight, and he moved cautiously, finally reaching the window. The sash wouldn't budge, and the warrior leaned close to the window. The single lock he could see was unlatched. The sash might be damp, the wood swollen, holding it closed. He tried again. Putty flaked away as he pushed up, but he felt some slight movement.

Trying once more, he managed to get the sash up far enough to squeeze his fingers under its bottom. This time he used all his strength, and the sash rose grudgingly, groaning in its channels, but finally opening wide enough for him to slip inside.

Once in the dark room, he stopped to listen. The house was silent. He could hear a faint, distant hum, but couldn't tell where it came from. Clicking on the light, he played it around the room. It was a bedroom, neat and Spartan—one chest of drawers, one bed and that was it. A rag rug lay on the floor beside the bed. Bolan dropped to one knee, peered under the bed, but saw nothing.

A closet in one corner caught his eye, and he moved toward it, the Beretta ready in his hand. He paused for a second with his hand on the knob, flattened against the wall beside the door, just in case. On the count of three, he jerked the door open, but the closet held nothing but a handful of hangers.

He cat-footed to the closed door and stopped once more to listen. No sound came from the other side of the door, and he tried the knob, which turned easily and soundlessly under his hand. Hearing nothing, he walked into the hallway.

Three more bedrooms comprised the rest of the second floor, and he entered the one at the end of the hall. His flashlight picked up something on the mattress of the bare bed, and as the warrior advanced, he realized what it was—blood, and lots of it. Someone had tried to clean it up, but there was plenty left. And no amount of cleaning would have taken away the holes in the mattress ticking.

The next bedroom was almost identical to the first. There was less blood on the mattress, but signs that the floor next to the bed had been scrubbed hard and not too long ago.

The last room was as pristine as the one he'd entered. It seemed almost eerie, so clean and undisturbed, after the two rooms he'd just examined. Leaving it behind, the Executioner moved to the head of the stairwell.

Bolan paused at the top step, clicked off the light and started down. The steps creaked under his weight. He had almost reached the bottom, when the room exploded. The warrior dived to the floor, skidding on smooth wood and slamming into a wall at the bottom of the stairwell.

The spears of light from an automatic weapon had come from somewhere across from the steps. Bolan held his breath, knowing that at any second the room might flood with light. He held the Beretta up and ready, and felt behind him with one hand. There was a doorway somewhere nearby, if he could just find it. His fingers felt along a wall, then found a heavy molding. To the left, nothing but air. Pivoting on his spine, he shoved his legs through the opening, then hooked his feet on the door frame and pulled.

Halfway through, he tried to get up. Another burst of fire ripped toward him, and he felt the sting of wood splinters and paint chips as the frame was hacked to pieces. He fired twice, trying to pick out the gunman behind the momentary flashes.

The hammering stopped, but there was no indication that he'd hit anyone. Taking advantage of the pause, Bolan scrambled through the doorway and ducked behind the wall.

As far as he could tell, it was a solitary gunman. But the only way to get to him was across the open room, and that was certain death.

He wasn't sure where he was, but could see the dull gray outline of a window a few feet behind him. Groping along the wall, he found some shelves, he reached up to grab a can of food and tossed it into the room. Gunshots rang out, and Bolan aimed behind the flash. He heard a grunt and fired again. The gunfire stopped, and a deadweight slammed into the floor.

Getting to his feet, Bolan eased toward the doorway, and reached through to click on the light. Half expecting an onslaught of hellfire, he held his breath. The room stayed quiet.

The Executioner could see the body on the floor, curled into a semicircle. He couldn't see the gunman's face, but it didn't really matter. He wouldn't recognize him anyway. He'd have to get Anna here to be sure, but it looked like he'd found Michael Ekizian.

And he'd found something more, he was certain. He just didn't know what it was.

15

Bolan took one last look at the body, then turned off the light and walked out of the house. He wished Martell hadn't gone back to Paris, because he knew there was a chance that the dead man wasn't Michael Ekizian. And if it wasn't, it would help to know *who* it was. But there was no help for it, and he'd have to rely on Anna Chirkizian, and hope that she was telling him the truth.

He understood her hatred. He had felt that same way about the men who had been responsible for his own father's death. And there was no hatred like it, that burning in the gut that gnawed at you, burned and never consumed, refused to give you the satisfaction of knowing that someday you would be gone and the pain would stop.

There was only one way to stop that pain. Bolan had done it with a high-powered rifle. There was a memory, though, that stayed in the body. And that memory enabled him to feel something of what Anna Chirkizian was feeling. He would tell her that, and she would be unable to believe him, but it was still true.

But if she could bring herself to believe it, maybe she would bare her soul to him, tell him what he needed to know.

But he wouldn't bet the farm on it. That was another aspect of the hatred, the refusal to accept help. Vengeance for a family member was a vengeance that demanded personal satisfaction. It did no good to pray for a hit and run, or a lightning bolt. You couldn't soothe it by paying someone else to do the job. You had to do it yourself. And Bolan suspected that Anna was, somehow and someway, hoping and scheming to get her chance. But as much as he understood, he couldn't stand by and let her jeopardize six innocent people, no matter how important her revenge might be to her, no matter how necessary to her own well-being. The plain fact was that Anna was in the way, and he couldn't permit it.

He walked back to his car, started the engine and headed toward the highway. Fifteen miles later he found the lane to Anna's uncle's farm, turned in and rolled slowly to a halt in the front yard. He knew something was wrong, and when he saw Don Marshack running toward him, a gun in his hand, he threw open the car door and slammed on the brakes.

"What's wrong?"

"Anna's gone."

Bolan got out of the car. "Gone?"

"She left a note saying she had something she had to do. I don't know how she did it, but she did. She's flat disappeared."

"You sure the note is from her?"

"It's her handwriting."

"She say what it was that she had to do?"

"No I called Martell, but he wasn't back yet. I left a message. He'll call here as soon as he gets it, I guess, but I think maybe we should go back to Paris."

"You think that's where she's gone?"

"Where else?"

Bolan shook his head. "I don't know. The more I learn about her, the less I understand her."

Marshack was beside himself, but he was trying not to show it. "I wish she had told me. I wish—"

"It's too late for that, Marshack. We have to figure where she's gone. She's liable to do something to get herself killed."

"She's a strong woman. You don't know her like I do."

"Strong, yes, but bullheaded, and she's playing with fire. You know that as well as I do."

"So what do we do?"

"We wait for Martell's call."

"That could be hours."

"It'll be hours either way. And if we're on the road, we'll still have to wait. Just because we're moving won't make time go any faster. And if we move in the wrong direction, it'll be time wasted.''

"I suppose you're right. So what happened at the safehouse?''

"It had been used, and recently. And someone was shot there earlier tonight. There was blood on two beds, and signs that someone had tried to clean up. But there were no bodies or hostages.''

"You don't think—''

"I don't know what to think. But there was somebody there, waiting. I don't know whether he knew I was coming, or if he was waiting for someone else. But he jumped me. I was hoping Anna could identify him. I think it might be Ekizian, the man Martell mentioned was on his payroll.''

"You killed him?''

Bolan nodded. "I wish I could have taken him alive, but I didn't know he was there. Not until it was too late. That place looked like a slaughterhouse. There were bullet holes all over. Whoever did it must be coming back, or else they didn't want the bodies identified. That's the only thing that makes sense. Maybe Ekizian planned to come back and get rid of the rest of the evidence. Maybe that's why he was there.''

"If that's who it was.''

"Yeah. If that's who it was.''

"Martell said he's going to ransack the files, see what he can find on Armenian Heritage.''

"The hell with the files. We need the people."

Marshack laughed, a bitter sound, devoid of mirth. "You don't give up easily, do you?"

"I don't know how to give up."

Marshack looked at an old windup clock on the wall. "I wish Martell would hurry up and call."

"Give him a chance. It will take some time for him to find anything."

"And where is Anna while he's looking? I can't stand this."

"You're going to have to get a grip on yourself, Marshack. You go off half-cocked, and you're no good to Anna. You need to stay hard."

"Yes, you're right. It's been a long time. Too long, maybe. I've lost that edge, the instincts."

"Then work on getting them back. You're going to need them."

Marshack stared at the phone as if trying to make it ring by sheer willpower.

Bolan understood the tension, and understood, too, that Marshack had forgotten how to deal with it. But he couldn't afford to be too tolerant. He was going to need the painter, probably before the night was over, and he wasn't about to depend on somebody who wasn't in absolute control of his emotions.

"You have to consider the possibility that Anna was lying to you, Marshack," he said.

The painter nodded. "I've thought about it. But if she was, she had her reasons. I have to give her that. I—"

The phone rang. Marshack dashed forward and picked it up. "Hello?" He covered the mouthpiece for a minute. "It's Martell."

"Let me talk to him." Bolan got up and accepted the receiver Marshack held out to him.

"Before you say anything, tell me what Ekizian looks like."

Bolan stared at Marshack while he listened to the description. "All right. Now, what've you got? Where?" While he listened, he mouthed to Marshack to get a map.

"Six o'clock...right. Bring us weapons. We'll need to make sure. And make sure nobody gets wind of it. No, don't do that under any circumstances. You bring a special weapons team, we'll lose the hostages. Why? Because somebody on your team is telling them everything that's going on. Yes, I'm sure."

He took the map from Marshack and smoothed it against his hip. "Listen, Martell, have you heard from Anna? She left and we don't know where she went . . . All right, see you at six."

"Well?"

"They're at an abandoned aerodrome. World War I vintage. About a hundred and fifty klicks from here."

"Is he sure?"

"He's sure."

16

Anna drove as if the devil were after her. She hadn't liked leaving Marshack like that, but he never would have let her go alone. If he had let her go at all. And she had to. He would never understand that, and there wasn't time to try to explain.

Everything was coming unraveled now. She had played a dangerous game. She knew that going in, knew that there was a risk, but it had all seemed so simple. On the inside she could see everything. She could move Hampirian like a chess piece, and the others, too. Sooner or later, she knew, she would find the man she wanted. And when she found him, it would be time for the last move.

She'd had to buy their trust. That meant doing some things she hadn't wanted to, such as sleeping with Hampirian and contributing ideas. She had thought she could control things, so the ideas were all right. Nothing would come of them. But something had gone wrong. Double-crossing Hampirian hadn't been quite as simple as she thought it would be. And she had been double-crossed herself. She didn't think Hampirian had done it. He was too much taken with her. He would never have suspected her. But someone had, and someone had let her make all the moves until, out of the blue— checkmate.

But there was no room in her future for that. It was time for the endgame. Maybe it would all come apart. Maybe she wasn't quite as smart as she thought she was. Or someone else was just a little smarter. And she thought she knew who. But proving it wouldn't be easy. She'd have to take a risk, expose herself, but it was that or watch it all go down the tubes, leaving her with nothing—not the satisfaction of revenge long savored, and not the peaceful life to which she was entitled.

All the way to Paris, her nerves played tricks on her. She kept watching the rearview mirror, convinced that someone was following her. She'd see a light, watch it for a while, then it would disappear. She would tell herself she had been imagining things, only to see it again, right on her tail.

She had to get to her apartment, but it wasn't going to be easy. She knew, and she thought the big American suspected, that the bullet that had killed Aram had been meant for her. But she couldn't explain why she knew that without having everything else spill out. And once that happened, the game would be over.

Part of her thought it was over as it was, but she wasn't quite willing to face up to the possibility yet. It was too soon. There was still a chance that she could get her revenge, and while there was a drop of blood still flowing through her veins, she would continue to try.

Once she got to Paris, she would have to be even more careful. It would be harder to watch her back, harder, too, to get away if someone was to follow her. She'd be locked into the last stage of her plan, and there would be no turning back.

Anna circled the block where her building was located. She wasn't sure, but there might have been a face in the window of her apartment. Maybe it was her nerves playing tricks, but maybe not. She went around the block again, just to be sure. The window this time was just a blank. She could see the bullet hole catching the streetlight and its fine web of cracks glittering in the darkness. The bullet hole told it all. A few inches, and she would have been taken out of play. A few inches the other way, and Aram would still be alive.

She parked the car two blocks away and got out slowly, keeping one hand in her pocket on the small Browning automatic. It was just a .22 target pistol, but it was all she could get her hands on until she got into her apartment.

As she stepped out of the car, she heard an engine idling somewhere. In the predawn darkness, her ears

were hypersensitive. She walked along behind the
hedge bordering an apartment building across the
street from her own. The leaves were soaked with the
rain, but it was worth the discomfort to be sure.

Anna kept between the building wall and the hedge
until she reached a low stoop. Here she would have
to expose herself for a few seconds to get across the
open space. She stopped just long enough to listen,
and could still hear the idling engine. A car sat at the
curb in the middle of the next block. A tight plume
of exhaust rose up in the humid air and mixed with
rags of fog. She could see a man at the wheel, but he
was just a shadow. She couldn't possibly recognize
him at this distance. He was reading a newspaper,
looking for all the world like a man with nothing on
his mind.

She tightened her grip on the Browning, felt for the
safety and checked once more to make sure it was
off. She watched the man in the car for several minutes. What the hell was he waiting for? She wanted
him to go, wished him away, but he remained there.
A door opened, its latch clicking loudly in the
morning darkness.

She saw a band of light spill out onto a lawn, then
disappear. The man in the car folded his newspaper
and turned around. A few seconds later, someone
appeared in the street, walked quickly to the car and
opened the door. When the interior light went on, she

breathed a sigh of relief. It was a neighbor, probably getting an early start for work.

The car pulled away, the driver turning on the wipers and gunning the engine. Then it was gone. The trail of exhaust already mingled with the fog, leaving no trace of the car's passage.

Anna darted across the open space and moved in behind the next section of hedge. She was going faster now, trying to work off the anxiety of her enforced wait. She knew it might make her careless, but there was no time to waste.

She finally reached a spot directly across from her apartment, and stood watching the window for several minutes. There was no sign that anyone was inside. The lights were out, and the curtain never moved. She checked up and down the block and saw no one. Nothing seemed out of place. No lights showed in any windows she could see.

Anna reached into her pocket for the front door key, took it out and pushed through the hedge. Dashing across the street, she ducked into the vestibule, inserted the key and opened the inner door. So far so good. She ducked out of the way and watched the street for a minute to make sure no one had followed her in.

Backing into the main room of the lobby, she took the Browning out and held it in her hand. She looked both ways, then decided that she would take the fire stairs rather than risk the elevator. On the stairs, at least she could run if she had to. She was getting more nervous now, and was getting angry at herself for letting her emotions get the better of her. She couldn't afford it. Not now. Not when she was so damned close.

She opened the door to the fire stairs, held it a few inches and listened. For a split second she thought she could hear someone breathing. It took her a minute to realize it was her own breath echoing in the concrete-walled stairwell. She shook her head and opened the door all the way.

Craning her neck, she looked up the first flight, but could see only as far as the first landing. It was empty. She moved into the well and let the door close behind her. At the first landing, she knew she was hyperventilating. Her head felt as if it was going to spin right off her shoulders. She hadn't known it would feel like this. All that time, feeding the hatred, she had imagined how cool and calm she would be. But she had barely begun, and her body was betraying her.

She took several deep, slow breaths, trying to get into that Zen zone that Don always talked about. It came, but slowly. Turning the corner, she eased up the second flight. On an instinct, she moved to the door and looked down the hall on the second floor. It was quiet, the night lights low, but bright enough to show her anyone lurking in a doorway.

One more flight, she thought.

Slipping around the corner, she kept on breathing deeply, trying to make sure her nerves didn't come back. She reached the last landing and stopped to listen. Moving to the door, she flattened against it and peered with one eye through the small window of wire-reinforced glass. The third-floor hall, too, was empty.

Almost home.

She opened the door with her left hand, trying to keep her grip on the Browning despite sweaty palms.

Shifting the keys in her left hand, she let the door hit her in the back and found the key to her apartment. As soon as she had it, she ran as fast as she could. The lock seemed to repel the key for a moment.

Ripping the door open, she reached for the light, slammed the door and leaned against it, breathing hard. She was getting out of control again. Swallowing hard, she put the keys in her pocket and moved toward the bedroom.

She turned on the bedroom light. The room was a shambles. Someone had been there.

Anna raced to the bed, tugged off the mattress and flipped it over. She let out a long sigh. The box was still there. She opened it, took out the envelopes and counted them. Six, each already addressed to Michel Martell. That was the right number. They had been overlooked.

A pair of audiotapes was in each envelope, each neatly labeled with date and place of recording. She counted the envelopes once more, then stuck them in her coat pocket. She was reaching for the target pistol when she heard something click in the living room.

Grabbing the gun, she ran to the wall and pressed herself flat against it. She heard the door close, the lock muffled as it clicked shut.

Holding the gun high, she backed away from the door. Whoever had searched the place must have been watching, waiting for her to come back. She worked the slide on the pistol and brought the muzzle down toward the door. She saw the toe of a shoe on the gray carpet and tightened her finger on the trigger.

A second later someone charged through the door. Anna fired, but missed. The crack of the pistol was deafening in the small bedroom. The man was already scrambling to his feet when she found him over the sights. She squeezed again. The Browning bucked in her two-hand grip, and the man staggered back, a bright red stain on his white shirt.

He clawed at his chest for a minute, then collapsed back against the wall, his head forward at a funny angle.

She moved toward the doorway, knowing in her gut it wasn't over. The gun felt heavy. Her hands were so slick with sweat that the checkered grip in her palm felt as if it had been greased. She waited, taking short, shallow breaths.

The second man charged into the room, and this time she didn't miss. The bullet caught him above the shoulder, severed an artery and sent him spinning around the room, spraying blood in every direction.

He staggered a step, tripped over the mattress, then fell heavily onto the floor. He tried to get up, but the blood continued to spurt out of him, taking the last of his life with it.

So, she thought, someone knew. But who? She moved closer, looked each man in the face and was surprised that she didn't know either of them. "Who in the hell are they?" she whispered. They weren't Hampirian's men. She knew that. She'd have seen them.

And it dawned on her slowly. "Haroun," she whispered. "The bastard...."

17

Anna took one last look around the apartment, unable to shake the feeling that she might never see it again. Even if she came out of it alive, there was a good chance that she would have to run for her life. The thought of leaving the business she had worked so hard to build didn't make a difference to her now. Vengeance was all that mattered. But the man she wanted to kill was already gunning for her.

The thought that she had lied to Marshack kept nagging at her, but she brushed it aside. After all, she thought, her whole life had been a lie. What was one more?

She held the Browning .22 in her right hand as she opened the door. The gun, with its cumbersome suppressor screwed in place now, was stuck in her belt, and she arranged her coat so she could get to it in a hurry, but she was due for a run of luck, and hoped she wouldn't need the Browning. At least, not yet.

She left the apartment and walked quickly to the fire stairs, yanked open the door and sprinted to the ground floor. This time, she went out the back. She would leave her uncle's old Citroën where she'd parked it and take her own car. There was a chance it was being watched, but she'd feel more comfortable behind the wheel of something familiar.

Crossing mental fingers, she eased into the parking lot, climbed in and stuck the key in the ignition. For a brief instant she hesitated before turning the key. Images of countless car bombs, a modern staple of television news and tabloid front pages, ran through her mind, but she pushed them away, telling herself that her time hadn't come yet. It would be an unkind God indeed who would let her get so close only to toss in a colossal monkey wrench at the last minute.

She started the car, holding her breath for an instant until she heard the familiar cough of the engine. The envelopes in her pocket were bulky, and she placed them on the seat before hooking her seatbelt. It was two blocks to the nearest mailbox, and she drove slowly along the curb, pulled up alongside the box and left the car running while she mailed the tapes. There was enough on them to nail Hampirian and Haroun to a large cross.

She thought of the tapes as her estate, and Michel Martell was her sole heir. Once they were in his hands, it wouldn't really matter much what happened to her. It was all there—conversations between Hampirian and Haroun, and a long, rambling confession of her own role. She had listened to the confession a dozen times. The voice was hers, but somehow the person on the tape didn't seem like her. She'd play parts of it over and over, trying to find some link to the person on the tape, but she could never quite manage it.

But that was all behind her now. There was a good possibility that in a few hours she would cease to exist and the woman on the tape become her, in memory and in fact. But that was okay. There was something admirable about that woman, something she felt herself lacking. She didn't like what she had become, but she knew it wasn't her fault. Hampirian and Haroun had transformed her that awful night in the basement of her home in Erivan.

She could see it now, as plain as day. Her father, his face bleeding, his nose broken, an ugly gash on his left cheek. Haroun stood there, a sick smirk on his dark face. He rubbed the muzzle of the pistol against her father's forehead, almost tenderly, like a child caressing a parent's fevered brow.

She had thought then that it would be all right, that somehow her father would be spared. But Haroun was implacable. He had long since passed through that gauzy veil between freedom fighter and bloodthirsty killer. He had discovered a taste for blood, and it now no longer mattered who he killed, or why, as long as he got his fix.

She hadn't known his name then. And when she saw him with Hampirian the first time in Paris, she thought for sure that he would recognize her. But he hadn't. She was one terrified face among a thousand. Haroun saw only his victims. Their families were as bugs, something you squashed with a clenched fist if you noticed them at all.

It was then the plan had been born. It had taken months to put it together. All those times in Hampirian's bed were her penance, she had told herself, her penance for a sin she hadn't yet committed, but would when she got the chance. The strange thing was that Hampirian seemed actually to care for her. She understood that he wasn't like Haroun, that he wasn't a monster, just a fool. But she needed the fool to kill the monster. And so she let him use her.

It had bothered her that she was unfaithful to Don Marshack. He would never have agreed to her wild scheme, so she had chosen to lie to him. He gave her every freedom, never questioned her and was content to know that she had some terrible secret that she was unable to share with him. But he loved her enough to think that the day would come when she trusted him enough, when she no longer saw her vulnerability as a flaw.

But that day had never come. And now there was a better than even chance that it never would.

Something had died in her the night her father died, when Haroun had smiled and pulled the trigger. She would never forget the horror, not of her father's body, but of the wall behind him. Blood and brain tissue spewed like vomit on the white paint, running in driblets down to the baseboard. A chunk of brain tissue, larger than her thumb, had given in to gravity and fell to the floor with a splat far louder than the gunshot. She could hear it still.

That had been the beginning. All she wanted now was for the end to come. And she had taken the one irreversible step by mailing the tapes. In twenty minutes she would use her key and enter Hampirian's safehouse. That was all she had planned. It was better to let impulse play a role—that made it fresher, more pleasing. She didn't want to carry out some long-stale scenario she had lived and relived a thousand times in her head. It was much better to do it this way.

Early-morning traffic was light. It was still a couple of hours before sunrise. She was almost certain Hampirian would be at the house. As simple as he was, he wasn't troubled by moral ambiguities. He slept like a fat, bearded baby. He even sucked his thumb in his sleep, leaving a little damp spot of drool on the pillowcase.

It made her smile to think about it, how she had teased him the first time, and how upset he had been. It wasn't fondness that made her smile, though. It was the cruel pleasure she had taken in hurting him just a little. It was like pushing on a thorn in a cat's paw. She could make him wince whenever she chose. He was so vain, and this was an embarrassing secret, one she could taunt him with.

The house was dark when she got there. She let the car drift past, slowing to a crawl but not stopping. She parked around the corner. It was a tree-lined street south of the city, a big old house on a street of big old houses. Hampirian had an apartment on the third floor of a huge gray affair that smelled of marijuana in the hallways.

She walked quickly, her sneakered feet silent on the damp pavement. The front door was always open. No one who lived here had anything worth stealing except for their stereo equipment, but all the neighbors had the same stuff, and there was no reason to worry about burglars.

Anna took the stairs two at a time, careful to make no noise, but anxious to get up to his apartment and wake him with the gun barrel in his ear. It was finally time to make it all whole again. It was time for symmetry to bring order into a chaotic world. She used the key carefully, knowing that he was a sound sleeper, but still wanting everything to go smoothly.

The door swung back without a sound. She smelled pilaf, the sticky air full of the scent of toasted rice and spices. Closing the door, she waited a moment to get her bearings. She knew the place as she knew the back of her hand, but he was so sloppy, there was always the chance that he had left a pile of books in the middle of the floor, or forgotten to put away the oud he couldn't play but loved to stroke while he chatted with the students, especially the young blond women who seemed drawn to him for some reason.

Placing each foot cautiously, she found her way to the short hallway without mishap. Feeling her way along the wall, she reached the doorway. The bedroom door was open, and she stood there listening to the rasp of his breathing.

The bed creaked once, and she thought he might be lying there in the dark, staring at her. She took the gun out of her pocket and tiptoed into the room.

She bumped the edge of the mattress with one knee. She could almost see him outlined there under the blanket, a bulk of shadow in the predawn gloom. Putting one knee on the mattress, Anna leaned forward, the gun outstretched. She wasn't going to shoot him in his sleep. She wasn't going to shoot him at all yet. Not here and not yet.

Anna shoved the muzzle hard against him and he grunted, but didn't say anything. She pushed again, expecting him to bolt upright, but he just lay there.

Then the light clicked on. She saw the ropes, the gag, and turned, but too late. Something caught her over the left ear and everything went dark. She was conscious only of the pain in her head and the floor rushing toward her.

When she came to, she was on the bed beside Hampirian, trussed up like him. Thomas Haroun was sitting on a chair, a smirk on his face.

"Good morning," he said. "I think I might have surprised you just a little."

She tried to curse him, but the gag was firmly in place. She turned her head to look at Hampirian, whose eyes were bugging out of his head. He mumbled something but the gag kept it in.

"We'll leave in a little while," Haroun announced. "You might as well get some sleep."

18

Bolan and Marshack parked the car well back in a wooded bottom, the rear bumper tilted toward the bank of a small creek that wound through the trees.

They had a little over two hours before sunrise. Martell was due any minute, and they hiked back to the road nearly three hundred yards, hoping they hadn't missed him. Marshack had said very little since leaving the Chirkizian farm. Bolan couldn't tell whether the painter was angry or not, and if so, at whom. The Executioner knew only too well that the kind of anger Marshack might be feeling could lash out at anyone, and the odds were pretty much against the most deserving object being chosen.

But Marshack was a logical man, and it was better to let him stew in his own reflective juices than try to convince him of anything. Left alone, he would eventually get where he had to go. Try to push him, and his energy would just focus on pushing back.

They were traveling uphill, and that gave them a slight advantage, because headlights on anything on the road would be above them by thirty feet or so, and easier to see. He kept one eye on Marshack and one on his footing. The patches of slick, brittle grass, glazed with dew, were treacherous underfoot.

The last eighty yards to the road were a straight shot, a rail fence on one side of the rutted lane, a row of cypresses waving in the cold breeze towering over the other. The aerodrome was less than a mile away, and it had been tempting to drive by, but the risk was hardly worth the scanty intelligence such a pass would yield. They would have to wait until Martell showed up. Once they were seen, they would have little time for anything but an all-out assault. There would be no turning back. At the moment they had no choice but to believe that six lives hung in the balance, and the scales were dangerously tipped against them.

Off to the right, the road wound downhill in a lazy, serpentine coil after cresting on a high rise more than two hundred feet above the surrounding flatlands. Bolan reached the end of the lane first and hung back, ducking in among the undergrowth rooted in the shelter of the cypress trees, and watched the rise. Martell ought to be moving down into the valley any second.

If things went according to plan.

"He better hurry up," Marshack said, looking at the sky. "We're going to lose the dark in less than two hours. Once the sun comes up, we've got a much tougher row to hoe.''

''He'll be here.''

''You seem pretty sure.''

Bolan didn't really want to talk, but he knew it would help Marshack ventilate his anxiety. ''I think he's a good man.''

''We're all good men, Belasko, even Hampirian. It just depends on whose yardstick you use to measure things.''

''I use a yardstick for only one thing, Don...to draw the line. It's way too late for me to start trying to distinguish shades of gray. I don't try, and I don't really care. But the line is different. You cross it, and you're in big trouble. Hampirian crossed the line the minute he invaded Walter Jason's home and took his hostages. From that point nothing he thought or meant would make a difference. And he shot a man to death on camera, just to make a point.''

''And how do you know when someone crosses that line?''

''If you have to ask, you'll never know.''

''Very Zen.''

''Whatever....'' Bolan saw the lights and pointed. ''That's got to be Martell.''

They watched the lights approach. As they drew near the bottom of the hill, the driver switched from headlights to parking lights. They stepped out of the brush and moved toward the road.

The urge to run out into the open was overwhelming, and Bolan sensed that Marshack was ready to succumb. He grabbed the painter by the shoulder. "Let him come to us," he whispered. "Just in case it's not him."

Marshack started to argue, but realized his companion was right and dropped back. Both men squatted. They could hear the engine now, and the lights were only intermittent, sometimes buried in the thick growth along the road. The engine sounded powerful, probably not that of a car.

Martell was supposed to bring weapons, and he might have gotten his hands on a van. But even that possibility wasn't enough to overcome Bolan's instinctive caution. A moment later, a gray van rolled by without slowing down. The warrior put the speed at about fifteen to twenty miles an hour, and there was no sign that the driver was looking for anyone. A moment later, it was gone.

"Son of a bitch rolled right on by," Marshack muttered.

"It wasn't Martell."

"Then who the hell was it?"

"I have no idea."

"So I guess we keep on waiting," Marshack said.

"There's nothing else we can do. But I have to admit I'm curious about that van."

"Chances are it was some of Hampirian's people. But I can't figure what could be in the van. Why was the driver being so careful?"

"Just didn't want to call attention to himself," Bolan suggested.

"Yeah. Or maybe he knew we were here."

"I don't think so."

"Maybe your boy Martell isn't what you think he is."

Marshack had a point, but the Executioner didn't even want to consider the possibility. Everything hinged on the Frenchman now. If he'd sold them out, they were finished. They'd be lucky to come out with their skins intact.

It was nearly ten minutes before a second pair of lights appeared on the crest of the hill. Bolan saw it first and tapped Marshack on the shoulder. "Here he comes."

"That's what you said last time."

This time, the driver left his headlights on. But they could hear the throb of the engine rising and falling as the driver coasted, stepped on the gas to recover a little speed, then coasted again.

"Whoever it is he's looking for something. Or somebody," Bolan said.

Near the mouth of the lane, the engine died out almost completely. They saw the headlights angle toward them, then wink off. As the small van rolled past, Bolan recognized Martell's profile behind the wheel.

"That's him," he said, ducking back out of the brush and moving after the van. Martell followed the lane, the van bouncing over the rutted weeds, the ruby wash of the brake lights splashing on the brittle leaves. The lieutenant stopped a few feet in front of Bolan's car, killed the engine and jumped out. "Sorry I'm late."

"You see anybody on the road ahead of you?" Bolan asked.

"No, why?"

"Because another van came by about ten or twelve minutes ago. Whoever was driving was going out of his way not to be seen."

Martell shook his head. "I didn't see a soul. You get a look at the driver?"

"Not really. You bring the artillery?"

"Such as it is."

"Let's see."

Martell moved alongside the van then opened the back with a key. "You have no idea," he said, "how difficult it can be to get an armorer out of bed after midnight. As it is, I had to promise him a week's vacation. He doesn't know I can't deliver on that, but at least I got some of what we needed."

He hauled a wooden crate toward him, smacked the lid with a fist and popped a board free. He tore the rest of the lid off with a screech of bending nails.

He handed the first weapon to Bolan. It was an FA MAS assault rifle, the current weapon of choice for the French armed forces. It was a high-performance weapon, and despite its strange lines, which led French soldiers to call it "The Bugle," it was one of the finest assault weapons in the world. "There's plenty of ammunition," Martell said.

In addition to a half crate of full magazines for the FAs, he also had a grenade launcher for one of the rifles, and half a dozen grenades for the launcher. "I wanted to get a sniping rifle, too, but had to leave without it. We'll have to make due with what we have."

Another crate held a Soviet-made RPG-7 rocket launcher and three projectiles. "Courtesy of Abu Nidal," Martell said, opening the box. "We hit one of his cells last year. He had three of these ugly devils, and we might need them. I checked some old army maps. The aerodrome is surrounded by half a dozen pillboxes. A regular poor-man's Maginot line, it seems. If they're using the base in a big way, they just might have some firepower in the pillboxes. It'll take a dead shot through one of the loopholes to take out one of those bastards. They're old, but they were built to last. There are two hangars on the airfield, both old, but you could hide a zeppelin in either one. It'll take us awhile to find the hostages on the base, unless they've got more men than we can handle. In that case we might as well shoot ourselves right now and save some ammunition.''

''We'll find them,'' Bolan said. He slung the FA over one shoulder, placed the RPG shells into a canvas sack, picked up the launcher and snatched several 25-round boxes for the FA.

He stood waiting while the other men parceled the weapons and ammo between them.

When the two men were ready, the Executioner gave the order.

''Okay, move out.''

19

Thomas Haroun sat in the corner as motionless as a block of ice, one foot propped on the five-gallon can of gasoline. It was all coming together for him now, and he was determined to maintain his composure. He had Hampirian and the woman out of the way. They could be disposed of at his leisure. He had four of the hostages. One more little harvest, and he'd have all six. Thinking of Hampirian, he permitted himself the slightest of smiles. The fat man was such a buffoon. All his histrionics, his bombast and his posturing, and what did he have to show for it?

Hampirian was an empty skin full of air, a dry husk fit only to be blown away by the wind. He was too soft. He didn't have the instinct, the willingness to spill blood, one needed. Haroun had them, and he had no doubt about it. In a few hours he would issue his own set of demands. Nothing too grand, but grand enough to get him what he wanted. Hampirian was a dreamer, a political lapdog, an idealist.

But politics was for imbeciles. Haroun wanted money.

He was playing with a stacked deck, and he knew the cards inside and out. All he had to do was to stand pat and rake in the pot. Twenty million dollars ought to do it. To Walter Jason, that was walking-around money. Add Aldretti and Charlton, and there was enough clout, financial and political, to net him twice that, if he wanted it. But there was no point in being greedy.

He watched the clock on the wall, listened to its steady clicking as the hands quivered and slowly advanced, notch by notch.

Haroun permitted himself an uncharacteristic moment of charity, wondering whether it was really necessary to kill Hampirian and the woman. Deep down, he knew it wasn't. Once he got the money, he would be as free as a bird. Hampirian couldn't touch him, neither could Anna Chirkizian. But that was really irrelevant. He wasn't going to shrink from a little blood, not because it wasn't necessary.

What Hampirian and the other dreamers like him didn't understand, was that killing wasn't something you did only when you had to. You did it when you could, because it was easy, and because nobody could stop you. That was what made you tough. That was what put the fear of God into people. And scared people were impotent. Thomas Haroun's secret was that he understood that single, simple principle better than everyone else. That was why he would succeed, and why he would walk away without a scratch, his pockets full of money, his back bent under the sheer weight of the wealth he would receive.

It was time to go.

He walked to the door, stopped to look in the full-length mirror for a moment and tugged on the sleeves of his leather bomber jacket. He wanted everything to look just right. He opened the coat for a second to settle the automatic in its holster, then put out the light and left the room. The walk to the car was quick. The van would already be on its way. One more little raid, nothing at all, really, and he would have a handful of bait for his money trap.

Haroun drove slowly, not wanting to call attention to himself. It took him twenty minutes to reach the parking lot. The van was already there. He left the car and locked it, tucking the keys behind the rear license plate, and walked to the van.

He opened the door of the van and slid in behind the wheel. Only two men accompanied him this time, but that's all it would take. This one was a piece of cake. Hampirian was spread too thin, and he didn't have enough men he could trust to guard the hostages.

The ride to the École d'Armenie was uneventful and unhampered by traffic at such an early hour. He pulled up in front of the building and got out, leaving the van running. The two men in the back of the van climbed out as soon as he opened the door, one handing him a suppressed Uzi, the weapon of choice for the raid.

Holding the guns under their coats, they filed up the steps and into the vestibule. Haroun had a key, and the door opened silently. He knew the hostages were in the basement, knew only three men were assigned to guard them. It would be like taking candy from a baby. And that, Haroun thought, was what Hampirian was, a fat baby.

He led the way into the library and sat in an overstuffed easy chair that smelled of dust and old books. He arranged the Uzi under his leg, so that it couldn't be seen easily. "David," he instructed, "go downstairs and get Hampirian's people. They'll probably want to leave one on guard. If they do, don't worry about it. I'll handle it."

Haroun looked around at the books. He spotted titles in more than two dozen languages. Hampirian had been collecting them for years. Everything anyone could possibly want to know about Armenia was covered—history, language, religion, mythology, costume. Ruins and archaeological sites had a few shelves. In one corner, Turkey, the black beast for all Armenians, had a half wall to itself. The collection was the backbone of the school.

Knowledge, Haroun thought, shaking his head. Savoog never understood that power and money made knowledge unnecessary. If you had enough money, you didn't have to know anything at all. He smiled.

Footsteps down the hall told him David Bozik was coming back. The two guards came in first, looking confused. They stood there with their hands at their sides, until one rubbed sleep from his eyes. "What's wrong?" he asked.

Haroun shook his head. "Nothing." He glanced at his colleagues, who stepped aside.

Moving his leg, Haroun brought up the Uzi. The two guards looked at him, aware of the gun, not knowing why he was moving it, or perhaps wondering why he had concealed it in the first place.

Haroun hefted the submachine gun then looked up at the ceiling. The sleepy guard followed his gaze. The sudden stutter of the Uzi, almost pathetically subdued in the book-filled room, nearly cut him in two. Haroun moved the muzzle just enough to fire a burst at the second guard, who was too stunned to do anything but raise one hand to his mouth. The 9 mm slugs made a small, rough-edged circle just below the bent elbow.

The killer stood and started toward the door. Almost casually, he stepped aside, waiting for his men to precede him. Then, almost as an afterthought, he emptied the magazine into their backs.

Stepping over the two still-twitching bodies, he bent to leave his Uzi on the floor and took David's.

Slipping the safety off, he moved down the narrow corridor to the basement stairs at the rear of the building.

He started down, cocking his head to listen. He didn't think the suppressed fire of the Uzi would have been heard, but he wanted to be sure. There was no point in having come this far only to let it slip away from him because he'd gotten careless.

Haroun turned to the claustrophobic stairwell and took the steps two at a time. The Jasons were in the back room, but he had to go halfway to the front of the building to get around the mazelike shelves full of books and magazines.

The last of Hampirian's men was sitting on a ladderback chair, his Uzi across his lap, under an old issue of a magazine, opened to an interview with Fidel Castro. The guard glanced up once, then went back to his reading.

Haroun stopped in front of him, reached down for the magazine and closed it. The guard looked up more in surprise than annoyance. Haroun nodded toward the locked door. "Open up."

The guard stood. He let the magazine slide to the floor, slipped the gun over his shoulder on its makeshift sling of packing twine and reached into his pocket for the key to a heavy padlock.

He opened the door and stood aside.

"You better come with me," Haroun said, nodding toward the open doorway.

The guard licked his lips and stepped inside, still shaking his head.

He moved across the floor and was halfway there when Haroun stepped into the room. He looked at Walter Jason, wondering just how much the man was worth. Maybe twenty million was too little. Maybe he could get more. Jason was a billionaire, after all. Jason started to get up, but Haroun shook his head. "Don't move."

"Gag them."

The guard seemed puzzled, but he looked around, found the cloths that had been used the last time on a small table in the corner and quickly knotted one over Edith Jason's mouth. He did the same with Walter Jason, then stepped back. "Blindfolds, too?"

"Not yet," Haroun replied.

He sprayed the guard with half the magazine. Edith Jason tried to scream, and Haroun clapped a finger to his lips, shaking his head. He looked at both their faces. They were terrified, and that's exactly what he wanted. He wanted them to know they were a gnat's eyelash away from instant death. He had to handle them alone, and this was the best way.

He walked to the table, found the blindfolds and set down the Uzi. He worked quickly now, no trace of nerves, no panic. When he had knotted the blindfolds in place, he hooked the Uzi over his shoulder, then took each captive by an arm.

"Just do as I tell you, and you won't be hurt. Come on, and be very quiet. Do you understand?"

Walter Jason nodded, but Edith seemed paralyzed. He repeated his question, this time digging his fingers into the flesh of the woman's upper arm. She shook her head then, and he said, "Good. Very good. This will all be over soon."

The Jasons stumbled up the steep, narrow stairs, Haroun between them, pushing Walter and dragging Edith. At the top of the stairs, he stopped them and ordered them to wait while he checked the rest of the first floor.

A quick survey of the carnage showed him that all five men were dead, his own two men and Hampirian's three guards. The fewer people who knew what he was up to, the safer he would be, and the more of the money he could keep for himself. The truth was that he wanted it all, and he would kill anyone who got in his way. He had probably always known that, but it was just beginning to sink in with all of its implications.

He felt his lips curling up in a slight smile, despite the quiet voice in his head that warned him to go easy, not to get overconfident, not to trip. He stood in the doorway looking at the bodies piled like cordwood among the books. The juxtaposition struck him as ironically appropriate.

Casually, almost like a man in a trance, he entered the library and retrieved the gasoline can. It took no time at all to pour it all over the books and the floor, saving nearly a gallon for the four bodies. He tossed the empty can aside, gave one last look, then stepped into the hall. He lighted a cigarette, took a puff and turned his back.

Walking back down the hall, he found the Jasons where he had left them. With their hands cuffed behind their backs, there wasn't much chance they would have tried to escape, but he was suddenly conscious that desperation was about to become a factor. And the problem with desperation was that it wasn't logical, it wasn't predictable.

He started to move quickly, sprinting toward the front of the house, the hostages stumbling along with him. Haroun flicked the cigarette into the library as he went past, ignoring the muffled whump of the igniting fuel. He hustled them out the front door and shoved them into the back of the van.

20

Bolan led the way through the windbreak. On the far side an open field stretched for nearly half a mile. On its southern edge, another winding course of trees separated the field from a sloping meadow. In the distance a patch of woods was all that separated them from the outermost reaches of the aerodrome.

The warrior turned left and stayed just inside the ten-yard band of trees until he reached the south end of the field. When he reached the edge of the meadow, he stopped and waited for Marshack and Martell.

"I think we should get in close to see what we're up against," he said when the other two joined him.

Martell looked at the sky for a moment. "We have less than an hour and a half of darkness left. Once daylight comes, we'll have a tough job getting close without being seen."

Bolan nodded. "Okay, let's double-time it. Stay in the trees until we reach the corner of the field. We don't know how many men we're dealing with, and we don't know what kind of weapons they have." He looked at Martell for moment, then said, "Or do we?"

"No, we don't."

"Let's go." Bolan broke into a dogtrot. Sparse undergrowth scratched at his clothing, and thorny vines reached out to hold him back, but he had found a comfortable rhythm.

By the time he had reached the far corner of the field, he'd opened a lead on his allies, and stopped to wait for them. Somewhere on the far side of the trees, he could hear the rumble of an engine. It sounded as if it were coming toward him, but in the predawn gloom, it was hard to be sure.

Then headlights speared toward him, almost as if he'd been their target, but there was no change in the rumble of the truck as he ducked. Martell almost stepped on him before he reached up out of the shadows to pull the Frenchman to the ground. Marshack dropped beside them.

"What's happening?"

"Don't know," Bolan whispered. "A truck turned up."

"They couldn't have seen us," Martell said, his voice equal parts conviction and hope. "Could they?"

"No, I don't think so."

"Maybe it's just a security patrol," Marshack suggested.

"Michel," Bolan whispered, "you're sure this is where the hostages are being held?"

"Not one-hundred-percent sure, no. But it was the best information I could get. I wanted to yank Ekizian in and sweat it out of him, but he hadn't been home in a couple of days. That meant something was about to happen, so I had his brother picked up. It took some squeezing, but we got a little juice."

"And this is it?"

"This is it, yes. But the brother is scared. I think he was telling the truth, as much of it as he knew. I just hope he's right."

"There is definitely something going on here," Marshack commented. "Something out of the ordinary."

The truck continued toward them, still in no hurry. It was less than a hundred yards away, when it turned slightly, still drifting in their general direction.

The truck came to a halt a hundred yards farther on. A door slammed, then another. Voices drifted to the three hiding men. "Wait here," Bolan said.

Marshack grabbed him by the arm. "Where the hell are you going?"

"I want to see what they're up to. I'll be right back."

"Let's all go," Martell suggested.

"No, this is what I do. We're not going to run the risk of blowing it all to hell when we're this close."

Marshack agreed only grudgingly. But Bolan didn't wait for him to settle down. He slipped into the trees and worked his way carefully through the tangled vines, using the glowing taillights of the truck as twin beacons.

The voices had stopped and been replaced by the clank of metal on metal. Then that, too, stopped. But as the Executioner drew closer, he heard what sounded like the sound of earth being cut by a shovel. Closer still, and he was sure of it. He could hear the grunts now, the thump of dirt being piled, the click of a shovel edge against a rock. Why were they digging?

One explanation reared up in front of him like an angry cobra. Graves.

He took a deep breath and moved closer, catching his foot in a tangle of vines, grabbing on to the smooth bark of a slender birch to keep himself upright.

The tree gave a little under his weight, its branches rattling a little.

"What the hell was that?"

Bolan held his breath.

"A deer, probably. Keep digging. This place gives me the creeps."

"It's not the place, it's the damn bodies," the other man said. "I don't like this. Not at all."

"It's not up to you to like it. Just do it."

The shovels started again. Bolan angled to the left a little, until he could pick out the shadows of the men backlit by the glow of the truck lights.

The warrior wasn't close enough to see anything but their shadows. As far as he could tell, it was just the two men.

He left his FA and the RPG on the ground, then he drew the 93-R and slipped off the safety. He didn't want to shoot, he didn't want to risk alarm, but if he had to, he wanted it as quiet as possible. He'd sacrifice the stopping power of the rifle in exchange for the silence of the Beretta.

The truck engine continued its unsteady rumble, helping to cover his muffled footsteps as he crept past the vehicle and started to move toward the edge of the trees. He wanted to get a look in the truck if he could manage it.

As far as he could tell, there was no one in the cab. It appeared to be just the two men. The Executioner was now close enough to spy an Uzi on the running board on the driver's side, its stubby black suppressor blending in with the shadows, but the sharper angles of the submachine gun unmistakable in the wash of ambient light from the taillights and parking lights. The interior of the cab glowed a pale green from the dash lights.

"How deep?" one of the men asked.

"Keep digging."

"I don't like this. Haroun is going crazy, I think."

"Haroun was always crazy. You ought to know that. It's too late to worry about it now. He'd kill us if we tried to leave."

"Not if we leave now. Just get in the truck and go."

"He'd find us."

"Not if we run far enough and fast enough."

"You don't know him like I do. Shut up and dig, will you. I want to get back."

The shoveling resumed. Bolan cat-footed to the very edge of the trees. He was past the men now, and they had their backs to the truck. He might be able to get to the far side of the vehicle without being seen. The longer he waited, the more likely they were to stop their work, so he took one tentative step out of the brush and made a dash for it.

Gaining the safety of the truck, he moved on the far side, keeping it between him and the grave-diggers.

Crouching behind the rear wheel of the passenger side, he waited. The wavering rhythm of the shovels was picking up its pace, as if the men were getting close to the end and were in a hurry to finish the job.

He heard the sharp stab of a shovel into soft earth, then a second. The shoveling had stopped, and the two men approached the truck. Bolan coiled himself, ready to make his move. He could see their feet under the tail of the truck now, one standing slightly behind the other. The hinges of the rear doors creaked, and one of the doors swung around the side of the truck, narrowly missing Bolan as he ducked. It struck the side of the truck with a hollow boom like a great muffled bell.

"Grab his ankles."

"You grab his ankles. I don't want to touch him."

"Look, we have to get this done and get back. If we take too long, Haroun will be here. We don't want that. We were supposed to do this hours ago."

"Fuck Haroun."

"You tell him. He killed Ekizian, you think he won't kill you?"

Something scraped on the truck bed then, and one set of feet shifted in closer to the tail of the truck. "Get his arms, I can't carry him by myself."

Then a thud. Bolan found himself staring into the wide, dead eyes of a chubby man with a beard. One side of the dead man's face was covered with dried blood, matted in the heavy whiskers. The body started to move as one of the two men backed away, still holding the corpse by its ankles.

"Another one, at least." The body moved away, hauled like so much waste for the renderer's truck, and disappeared.

A second body was dragged out of the truck, its head cracking the ground with a dull thud. Bolan hadn't recognized the first man, and the second was just as unfamiliar. He breathed a sigh of relief when neither body was Anna, but there could be more bodies in the truck.

He was going to make his move as soon as the men came back. He listened, half expecting to hear the sound of the shovels again, but instead he heard the footfalls of the Armenians. He watched the ground just behind the truck. As soon as he saw both pairs of muddy shoes, he leaped out from behind the wheel, leveling the gun.

"Don't move."

One of the men went for his side arm, and Bolan fired once. The silenced 9 mm slug found its target, drilling into the man's left shoulder, and he went down hard. He still clawed for his weapon, forcing Bolan to fire a second shot. A third wasn't necessary.

The Executioner stepped toward the survivor, Beretta in hand. The man backed up a step, tripped over his dead friend and fell to the ground.

He made no attempt to move, instead lay there and stared at his dead companion, shaking his head.

"Get up," Bolan barked.

The man tried rise, but he seemed unable to control his muscles. Bolan took a step forward, reached down to grab him by the shoulder and hauled him to his feet.

The Executioner gave him a shove and steered him toward the trees.

21

Bolan's prisoner was terrified. He kept looking back over his shoulder, even though it was still too dark to see. He tripped and fell, and the Executioner had to reach down and drag him to his feet again.

When he reached the place where Martell and Marshack had concealed themselves, he pressed the man to the ground. Martell stepped closer. "Who is he?"

"I was hoping you could tell me."

"Where is Savoog Hampirian?" Martell asked.

"In the hangar."

"How many men does he have with him?"

The man started to laugh. "None."

"What's so funny?" Marshack demanded.

The man shook his head and refused to answer. Marshack stepped closer and drew back his fist. "I asked you a question."

Martell stepped between them. "Leave him alone.

We can't beat the information out of him. There's no time.''

"I won't take long."

"How many men does Hampirian have?" Martell repeated, his voice this time sharp-edged and impatient.

"None."

"You're lying."

"No. You're on the wrong trail."

Bolan was getting interested. As near as he could tell, the prisoner was the man who had expressed the desire to get away. He knelt in front of the man. "You mentioned someone named Haroun when you were digging the graves. Who is he?"

"Haroun?" Martell asked.

Bolan nodded, but never took his eyes off the prisoner. "Is Haroun in charge now?"

The man nodded.

"How many men does he have there?"

"Ten, twelve, something like that. And he had some with him."

"You mean he's not there now?"

"No. Not yet. Any minute."

"Where is he?"

The man swallowed hard, but didn't answer.

"You don't like Haroun much, do you?"

The man shook his head.

"You'd like to get away from him, wouldn't you?"

"He's a madman. Yes, I would like to get away. So would you, if you were in my shoes."

"But if you help us, if you tell us what you know, we'll get him. Then you won't have to worry about him anymore."

"No. He will find me. There is nothing you can do to stop him. He is a crazy man. No one can stop him."

"If you don't tell us what we want to know, we'll make sure he does find you. Your only chance is to cooperate with us, and we don't have time to play games with you."

The man seemed to be thinking it over. Bolan changed the subject. "The bodies you were going to bury. Haroun killed them?"

"Yes."

"Were they Americans?"

"No. Not Americans, Armenians."

"He killed some of his own people?"

"More will die. Professor Hampirian. The woman."

Marshack bolted forward. "What woman? Anna Chirkizian? Where is she?"

"I don't know her name. Long black hair. Very pretty. She was at Hampirian's. Haroun said he knew she would be there, so he waited for her. Then we brought her and Hampirian to the hangars.''

''Where is he now?''

''Getting the other Americans.''

''Why?''

''He—'' The man stopped and shook his head.

''You have to tell us,'' Bolan prodded. ''If anything happens to the hostages, it'll be on your head.''

''Haroun wants money. He doesn't care about the political prisoners. He's going to kill them all, but he wants the rich one, Jason, to make a tape first, asking for the money. He'll keep Jason alive until he gets the money.''

''When is he planning to do this?''

''Today. As soon as he gets here. He's bringing Jason and his wife.''

''From the school?''

The man nodded.

''That doesn't give us much time, Belasko,'' Marshack said. ''We have to move.''

''We can't do anything until he gets here. Once all the hostages are here, then we can make our move.''

''But Anna's—''

''Marshack, this isn't just about Anna, do you understand? This is about the hostages, too. She's in deep and brought this on herself. We'll save her, but the hostages have to come first.''

"I agree," Martell said. "They must be our first concern."

"Damn you both!" Marshack turned away. He was angry, but he knew Bolan was right. Especially about Anna having made her own bed. He knew that, had been afraid of it all along, but he just hadn't allowed himself to accept it. It had been easy to push it aside before. Now he had no choice.

He took a deep breath, then turned around. "All right. What are we going to do?"

"Our friend, here, is going to tell us everything he knows. Where Haroun's men are, where the hostages are being held, where Anna and Hampirian are, defenses, weapons, you name it. Once we have that information, we can see where we go next." He turned to Martell.

"You have that map of the aerodrome?"

The lieutenant nodded, removed the map from his pocket and spread it on the ground in front of the captive.

"Show us everything you know, and make it fast," Bolan told his prisoner.

"I can't read maps. I—"

Bolan stabbed a finger at the paper. "These are the hangars. Which one are the hostages in?"

"They're not. Only Hampirian and the woman. The hostages are in a—what do you call it—a bunker, a fort? There are many of them here."

"A pillbox?"

The man nodded. "Yes, a pillbox."

Bolan bent close to the map. "There are six of them. Which one? Are they all in the same one?"

"Yes, all in one. Close to the hangar." He looked at the map. "Here. There is a tunnel from the hangar to the pillbox. The men are in another pillbox, this one here, except for those watching the professor and the woman."

"There is a network of tunnels," Martell said. "All the pillboxes are connected underground, to one another and to the hangars. There was a barracks, also connected, but it is gone now."

"Has the opening been bricked over?"

"What do you mean?"

"Where the barracks was. If it was connected, the tunnel is still there. If we can get in that way, we can get into the hangars."

Martell looked dubious. "I don't know. There is nothing on the map to tell us."

Bolan looked at the captive. "What about it?"

"I don't know."

"It's our best bet," Marshack said. "Let's just check it out."

"Maybe one of us could go," Martell suggested.

Bolan vetoed the idea. "We can't run the risk of splitting up. If we lose one man before we start, we might as well pack it in. Not only do we tip them off, but we raise the odds. They're too high as it is."

"We better do something before the sun comes up," Marshack said.

"Okay, let's go," Bolan said, picking up the map.

"What about him?" Marshack asked, jabbing a finger at the captive.

"We can't let him go now. He'll have to come with us."

"No, I cannot."

"We can spare a bullet," Marshack suggested.

"No," Bolan said flatly. He looked at the captive. "Is there rope in the truck?"

The man shrugged.

"Marshack, check it out."

The painter grumbled, but did as he was told. Three minutes later he was back, a coil of rope in his hand. "This should take care of it."

"Tie him up and gag him," Bolan ordered.

"What about the truck? We can't just leave it here."

"Load the gear. We'll use the truck to get as close to the hangars as possible. With any luck, it'll cover us while we try to get into the tunnels."

Marshack grabbed Bolan by the shoulder. "You do know just how long a shot this is, don't you?"

The Executioner looked at the man for a long, silent moment. "You bet I do," he said.

22

The ruined brick foundation of the barracks was clearly discernible in the headlights of the truck. Bolan braked just beyond it, leaving the truck between the foundation and the nearer of the two hangars. He killed the engine and the lights, then climbed down from the cab. The pillbox with Haroun's men was on the opposite side of the hangars, and there was no danger of being seen if they worked quickly.

According to the prisoner, security was lax, at best. Haroun was convinced that no one knew where they were, and he was arrogant enough to believe that an occasional sweep around the perimeter of the Fleury Aerodrome was sufficient.

They didn't have anything so grand as a plan. They were flying by the seat of their pants. Martell was concerned, and Marshack was reckless enough not to give a damn. But Bolan wanted to take it step by step. Getting into the tunnels was the first priority. After that, they'd just have to wing it.

Weeds sprouted all over the place. Vines, killed by the cold weather, were tangled in the bleached and splintered timbers. The barracks had been razed, but half of the debris was still there, some of it stacked and some just lying on the ground among the weeds. They were looking for a metal hatch that dropped straight down a dozen feet, then led toward the hangars and on to the pillboxes in a network of brick-lined catacombs.

They couldn't use lights, and Bolan split them up, assigning each a third of the foundation edge closest to the hangars. The warrior took the left-hand corner of the ruined barracks.

The hangars loomed up like gray mesas in the predawn darkness. Bolan glanced once at them, pitch black and shapeless domes, then got on hands and knees, the FA scraping the ground as he slid timbers aside and pawed through the weeds.

Marshack was next to him, feeling the ground with flat palms as if smoothing paint on a canvas. Martell was more methodical, clearing weeds, then leaning close to look for any telltale sign of the hatch.

Bolan found it.

The hatch had rusted over and refused to budge when the warrior tugged on the metal handle. Marshack and Martell leaned over his shoulder, the painter grabbing the handle and helping to pull.

"I saw an iron bar," Martell whispered. "Maybe we can use it to pry the hatch loose." He moved away and raked the weeds with his hands once more, found the bar and sprinted back.

It was useless as a pry, but small enough to slide through the handle. Bolan braced it against the concrete frame on the far side and levered the bar upward. The hatch still wouldn't budge.

"Hurry, I see a light," Martell whispered.

Bolan glanced to where the Frenchman was pointing and saw the wavering beam of flashlight. "Must be the sentry."

He put his back into the bar, and Marshack stood on the other side and pulled. The hatch started to grind in its seat, and finally came away with a crack as the corrosion gave way. It was heavy, and it took the two men to muscle it to one side.

Bolan peered down into the hole, as black as a well, groped with one hand and found an iron ladder. He lowered himself into the shaft and reached back for the RPG and the canvas sack. He dropped down quickly, then turned on his flashlight, training it on the bottom of the ladder.

Marshack came next, followed by Martell, who paused long enough to pull a couple of rotted boards over the hatchway. They stood in a concrete chamber that stank of age and decay.

Bolan played the light around and found the entrance to the tunnel. It was nearly six feet high, but both he and Marshack had to duck to enter it.

Playing the light ahead of him, Bolan took the point. The walls were lined with brick, and lichens the color of patinated copper had overgrown the masonry joints. It was nearly two hundred yards to the nearer of the two hangars. Double-timing it in a crouch, Bolan picked up the pace, counting steps until he came close to where the hangar was, a dozen feet above them.

Bolan moved slowly now, looking for the side shaft that led to the first hangar. Twenty feet ahead, he found it. "All right," he whispered, "that's one. Let's have a look at that map, Michel."

Martell spread the map on the floor, and the three men crouched over it. Bolan stabbed a dusty finger at the map. "We're just about here. The next hangar is about two hundred yards dead ahead."

He traced the broken line representing the tunnels. "We go past the second hangar, then we have a semicircle. It looks like maybe four hundred yards here, connecting the first cluster of pillboxes. According to what our prisoner says, the hostages are in the middle one. Haroun's men are all the way at the end of the semicircle. There's only three of us, so I think our best bet would be to get the hostages first, bring them down into the tunnel and get them to the hangar.''

"They're guarded," Marshack reminded him. "So is the hangar."

"Right, but if we can get them out, then we can take on the guards in the hangar. That'll put us farther away from the rest of Haroun's men."

"We don't know where Haroun himself is," Martell said.

"True, but we do know that he plans to kill Hampirian and Anna when he returns. Chances are he'll go first to the hostage bunker to drop off the Jasons. If we can take him there, it would be best. If not . . ."

He let the thought hang in the air. It wasn't necessary to verbalize it, but Marshack wouldn't let it rest. "If not, then maybe he beats us to the hangar. Maybe he murders Anna before we get there to stop him."

"There's no other way. You know it as well as I do."

"I could stay at the hangar, just in case."

"No. It'll take all three of us to get the hostages out."

"What about the rest of Haroun's men?"

"If they don't know about the tunnels, and we have no way of knowing whether they do or not, we can take them on last, once the hostages, Hampirian and Anna are safe.''

"And if they do know about them?"

Bolan took a deep breath. "If they do know about them, things will get very interesting before this is all over."

"There is another way," Martell said. "If we just get the hostages and Anna, we can get them into the truck. We can move them, then come back. I can call for a tac squad at that point, one of our antiterrorist units."

"Maybe. But that assumes we can get them out without alerting the others. It's worth a shot, but we have to plan for the worst case."

"All right, let's do it your way," Martell said.

"Marshack?" Bolan asked.

"You're the boss."

"Let's do it, then."

Martell folded the map, tucked it into his coat and stood. Bolan took the point a second time. They were moving quickly, painfully aware that they had no way of knowing what was happening on the surface. Once they got to the pillbox where the hostages were being held, they would have to try to judge whether the Jasons had been added to the group. It would be best if they got there before Haroun. If they opened the hatch too soon, it would ruin everything. But if they waited too long, Anna Chirkizian was doomed. Circumstances were shaving the time to split seconds. Timing would make all the difference, and at the moment they were flying blind.

They reached the end of the semicircular tunnel in five minutes. So far, only rats and spiders knew they were there. Bolan hoped to keep it that way for another half hour.

He was watching the wall now, looking for the ladder that would signal they were under the first, vacant pillbox. According to the map, it should be about seventy or eighty yards along the curving wall.

It was right where it should be.

"What are we stopping for?" Marshack hissed.

"I want to see how the hatch works. My guess is they're all the same. It could make a difference." He started up the ladder. The hatch was hinged, and dropped back away from the ladder. Held in place by a dog at either free corner, it would swing down of its own weight, if it wasn't rusted—and if it wasn't locked from the other side, a possibility they hadn't anticipated.

Bolan worked the dogs loose and grabbed the handle. He was trying to make as little noise as possible, to see just how quietly it could be done. Pushing up with his right hand, he pulled down on the handle with his left. There was a slight scraping sound, but the hatch opened easily. He let it fall all the way, then moved up the ladder far enough to poke his head into the pillbox.

Sweeping the interior with the light, he found himself scouring seamless concrete walls. The pillbox was a single chamber shaped roughly like a loaf of bread. Thirty feet by ten or twelve, it was closer to the inside of a tomb than anything Bolan hoped to see for a while. Oblongs of gray spaced along one wall showed him where the sky was brightening beyond the loopholes.

He'd seen enough, and it wasn't encouraging. Bullets fired inside the pillbox could ricochet several times. With six hostages milling around, there was a chance that one or more of them might stop one. But it couldn't be helped.

He closed the hatch and descended the ladder.

"Well?" Martell asked.

"It'll be tight. There's no margin for error, I can tell you that. Once we open the hatch, we're not going to have much time—ten, maybe fifteen seconds. There's no place to hide in these damn things." Bolan glanced at the FA on his shoulder. Good as it was, he hoped he didn't have to use it. He checked the Beretta and the Desert Eagle.

"There's only one way to do it," he said.

"What's that?" Marshack wanted to know.

"One of you will have to go on to the last pillbox, get on the other side of the hatch. The other will be halfway between the second and the last. That man can cover my back when I go up. Together, you can squeeze Haroun's men, if they know about the tunnels and if they come down into them."

"I don't like the idea of your going in alone," Marshack said. "It's too risky."

"There's no other way. Only one man at a time can take the ladder. A second man would have to wait for me to get up and into the bunker anyway. Once that happens, the war is over either way. They get me, or I get them. There's not going to be any middle ground."

"But—"

"That's all she wrote, Don. There's no other way."

Bolan didn't wait for an argument. He aimed the light down the tunnel and moved on. The second ladder was nearly a hundred and fifty yards away.

The Executioner climbed the ladder and pressed an ear against the hatch. He could hear talking on the other side. The words were nearly drowned in echo. But he could hear enough. "That's the last of them," someone said. "I'll be back in half an hour. I have some unfinished business then I want to tend to the esteemed Professor Hampirian and the Chirkizian bitch."

Bolan climbed back down and checked his watch. "Haroun's just leaving," he whispered. "You've got three minutes, Don."

Marshack was already sprinting, his light bobbing up and down along the lichen-covered bricks. Bolan watched the hands on his watch, then headed back up the ladder as Martell drifted away from him.

Bolan was alone in the dark.

And it was time.

23

Bolan loosened the last dog on the hatch, took hold of the handle and pulled hard. It resisted for a moment, then came free with a soft grinding sound. He held it open for a few seconds, listening for some sign that he had been heard.

On five, he let the hatch all the way down. Light from the pillbox spilled down through the opening. He could hear voices clearly now. He wished for a moment he knew how many hardmen were on-site, but it was an idle thought. The die was cast. He went another rung up the ladder, ducking to keep his head below the floor level.

The Executioner peered over the rim and spotted one guard immediately, standing ten or twelve feet away, his back to the hatch. The second was on the far side, next to Norman Charlton. A third sat on the floor against the wall at the other end of the row of hostages, who sat on folding chairs, their hands behind their backs, most likely handcuffed or tied.

Before the warrior could make a move the guard sitting on the floor gave a shout of alarm and clawed for his side arm.

The Executioner snapped off a shot from the silenced Beretta, drilling the guard through the forehead. The man directly in front of Bolan must have heard the spit of the 93-R because he turned, but he was looking too high, and Bolan fired again, the 9 mm slug catching him under the chin and punching him backward before depositing him on the floor in a heap.

Bolan had pushed himself up and out the hatch before the last guard realized what was happening. He swung an M-16 the Executioner's way, but too late. The third death messenger from the Italian automatic shattered a rib and plunged on through his heart as he tried to turn.

The hostages were gagged and blindfolded, but they knew something was wrong. Bolan ran across the pillbox floor. He was going to need help, and Aldretti was his best bet. He took the former NATO man's blindfold off, held a finger to his lips, removed the man's gag and whispered, "Are you all right?"

Aldretti nodded.

Bolan leaned forward, saw the handcuffs and asked, "The key?"

Aldretti looked around then, saw the guards and nodded toward the man sitting on the floor, whose head was now slumped on his chest. Bolan went to the dead guard, searched his pockets and retrieved the key. Seconds later, Aldretti was free. "All right, listen, there's not much time, so I don't want any screwups." He shoved the key into Aldretti's hand. "Turn the others loose. No noise. Got it?"

The man nodded.

"Get everybody down into the tunnel. I'll meet you there as soon as I can." He took the M-16 from the dead man's hands and tossed it to Aldretti. "Don't use this unless it's a last resort."

Bolan had almost reached the hatchway by the time Aldretti said, "I got you."

The warrior dropped into the tunnel and joined Marshack and Martell.

"So far so good," he said, when the three of them were together.

"What next?" Marshack asked.

"We get the hostages out of here. The hangar is our next stop. Haroun might already be there, but it sounded as if he had something else to do first. We'll get Anna out if we can...."

They were sprinting back toward the hostage pillbox. By the time they reached the ladder, Aldretti was already on the floor. Charlton was on the way down, and above the man's head Bolan saw a pair of women's shoes. One by one the women came down the ladder, Charlton helping them from below, and Walter Jason from above. Charlton had a pistol tucked in his belt now, probably belonging to one of the guards. Jason carried an Uzi.

When all six were on the floor, Bolan said, "We're not out of the woods by a long shot. They have another prisoner, and we want to get her out. If you make any noise, it could cost us."

Jason and Charlton looked grim. Aldretti was ready for anything, the former military man's combat instincts already rekindled. The women wore blank stares, their eyes glazed over.

"Any questions?" Bolan asked.

There were none.

"Let's go."

Marshack and Aldretti took the lead, while Bolan and Martell hung back to cover the rear. As they started to move, a light speared down the tunnel from the direction of the last pillbox. The beam struck Martell for a moment, and he hit the deck.

A burst of gunfire exploded at the far end of the tunnel, sending a shower of brick shards and bullet fragments in every direction.

"Go, go, go!" Bolan opened up with the FA, lacing a tight figure eight toward the flashlight beam. It went out, but too late. The gunner went down, but the damage was done. Martell got to his feet and Bolan covered him. The tunnel would be full of Haroun's men in no time, unless they did something to prevent it. Backing up was useless, there was no place to hide in the narrow tunnel. The two sides could trade firebursts and cut each other to ribbons. The winner would be the side with the most targets, not the most weapons.

Bolan started forward.

"Where the hell are you going?" Martell shouted.

"We have to stop them here, or lose it all. You get out of here. Get Anna if you can, but get the hostages out at all cost."

"You can't do it alone, Belasko."

"Just go!"

Bolan charged ahead, knowing that the next man down the hatch could take him out just by sweeping the tunnel with a blind burst. He kept to the wall, moving as fast as he could. A block of light on the tunnel floor far ahead told him the hatch was open, but nothing else.

As he ran headlong, his shoulder brushing the brick on his left, he saw the light smear, then disappear for a moment. He cut loose with the FA, and a body fell to the floor.

Fifty yards to go, and so far, so good. The light grew dim again, and Bolan could see someone leaning down through the hatch. The gunner was trying to keep his balance and bring an Uzi under control at the same time. Bolan chipped away with the FA, sending the gunman ducking back up into the pillbox.

He was ten yards away when the man ducked through again. This time, a burst from the FA splattered him all over the wall behind the ladder.

Bolan dropped to one knee and swung the RPG-7 off his shoulder. He rammed a projectile home when someone dropped straight through the hatch, not bothering with the ladder. The warrior grabbed for the FA and rolled, just avoiding a burst of Uzi fire. He threw the FA, caught the gunman on the shoulder and sent him reeling. It bought Bolan time, and he hauled out the Beretta as the man recovered. One shot punched the gunman in the chest, knocking him back, and sending the Uzi rolling off into the dark.

Watching the hatch, Bolan retrieved the FA and rammed in a new clip. The men above were like bees in a hive, and a single break was all they needed. It was Bolan's job to see to it that they didn't get that break. He raced back to grab the RPG-7. As he started up the ladder, he saw a face appear over the hatch, and he jabbed the RPG like a spear, hitting the unsuspecting terrorist in the eye and drawing a roar of pain. Bolan aimed the RPG through the hatch and dropped from the ladder.

He ran like hell, changing clips in the FA and letting it all go in a continuous burst. The rocket went off at the same instant, sending a choking cloud of dust rolling down the tunnel. The ground rumbled, and the warrior could sense that the walls wouldn't hold.

Bolan turned it on as the first bricks started to bulge out of their courses. Hunks of the ceiling clattered to the ground. For good measure, he turned, let a second rocket go and hit the deck. The concussion rolled over him, and his ears rang as the rocket went off. He felt his shirt flap, then heard the rumble of the tunnel walls collapsing.

There was no time to see if the tunnel was blocked, and Bolan scrambled to his feet. He couldn't hear, and he felt light-headed, but he kept on running. He used a light now, so he could run flat out. He reached the end of the tunnel and scrambled up the ladder into the morning light. The last of the hostages was climbing into the truck. Martell saw him.

"Where's Marshack?"

"The hangar."

"Let Aldretti drive the truck. We have to go back."

Steven Aldretti jumped down from the truck and looked at Bolan. "You all right?"

Bolan shrugged. Martell helped him out of the hatch. They sprinted across the open ground now. The hangar looked less imposing in the gray light of a rainy dawn, but it was still enormous. A side door was open, and the Executioner headed right for it.

Gunshots rang out. "Haroun!" he shouted. His voice boomed back at him from every corner. It was still near dark inside the building, and it seemed to mock him as the echo of his shout dwindled away.

He heard the crack of a pistol off to the left. He started to run, hoping it wasn't too late. A clang echoed through the hangar and light flooded one end. Bolan saw a string of floods mounted on a girder, and a jumble of cartons cascading from one corner of the huge building.

Near the end of the building, he saw Don Marshack, sprawled on the floor and trying to sit up. Beyond him, two bodies lay sprawled in ignominious death. Marshack had made a good start. A gun cracked again, and sparks flew as a bullet glanced off the concrete floor just to Marshack's left.

There was another shot, then another. Marshack screamed, "No, Anna, no!"

"Not yet," Haroun roared, his voice distorted into a rumble by the cavernous hangar.

"You can't get out, Haroun," Bolan shouted. Another shot greeted his voice, and sparks flew again, this time just behind Marshack. The whine of the slug died away. Marshack tried to get up, but one leg of his jeans was soaked with blood, the effort was more than he could manage. Bolan and Martell sprinted past him.

"Stay with Marshack," Bolan instructed, and Martell skidded to a halt. "Get him out of here."

Tall shelves concealed one corner of the hangar, and Bolan knew that Haroun had to be somewhere behind them. But he couldn't risk a shot until he knew where Anna was. Haroun spotted him and cut loose with a suppressed burst, the lethal hailstones pelting the floor all around Bolan as he sprinted to the nearest cover.

"Give it up, Haroun! We have the hostages. You have nothing left to win."

"Go to hell," the Armenian shouted.

Bolan crouched behind a huge stack of steel drums. He rapped one with his knuckles, and it tolled hollowly.

"I know where you are," Haroun taunted. As if to prove it, he fired a sustained burst that rattled into the drums.

"And I know where you are."

"But I have the woman. You want the woman. I know that."

"That's right, I do. What about Hampirian?"

Haroun laughed, which told Bolan all he needed to know. Savoog Hampirian was dead.

The Executioner caught a glimpse of movement. Peering between two drums, he could see one leather-clad arm resting on a shelf between two wooden crates. He took aim with the FA and fired a short volley, trying to punch through the crates. But whatever was inside them stopped the slugs before they could get to Haroun.

Bolan upended one of the drums and gave it a kick. It went rolling and bouncing across the floor, drawing Haroun's fire and his attention. The warrior launched a second drum, and this time sprinted to the left while Haroun wasted ammunition on the empty canister.

Juking to the left, the Executioner reached the wall of the hangar. He squeezed past the shelving and saw Anna Chirkizian, bound and gagged, sitting on a wooden chair. Next to her, Savoog Hampirian slumped back against the wall, his shirt a brilliant red. What had been his face was no longer recognizable as human.

Haroun was at the other end of the rank of shelves, his attention still fixed on the drums.

The warrior stepped out and leveled the FA. "Haroun," he barked. The echo of his voice confused the terrorist, who whirled, weapon tracking, trying to find him. He slipped away from cover, and Bolan squeezed the trigger.

When the echo of the gunfire died, Thomas Haroun lay still.

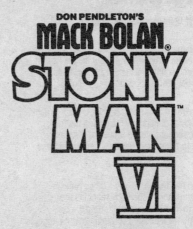

Follow the exploits of a crack direct-action unit in the
thrilling new miniseries from Gold Eagle . . .

SLAM

by DAN MATTHEWS

The President just unleashed the big guns in the toughest offen-
sive of the war on drugs—SLAM, the ultrasecret three-man strike
team whose mandate is to search-locate-annihilate the threat
posed by multinational drug conspiracies.

In Book 1: **FORCE OPTION,** a dangerous Mexican-Colombian
axis forged by two drug kingpins ranks priority one for the SLAM
team—a team that extracts payment with hot lead.

A new age of terrorism
calls for a new breed of hero

NOMAD

S M A R T   B O M B

D A V I D   A L E X A N D E R

Code name: Nomad. He is the supreme fighting machine, a new breed of elite commando whose specialty is battling 21st-century techno-terrorism with bare-knuckle combat skills and state-of-the-art weapons.

Desperately racing against a lethal countdown, Nomad tracks a rogue weapons expert but runs into a trap. He comes face-to-face with his hated nemesis in a deadly contest—a contest in which the odds are stacked against him.

Meet Jake Strait—a modern-day bounty hunter in the ruthless, anything-goes world of 2031.

by FRANK RICH

Jake Strait is a licensed enforcer in a world gone mad—a world where suburbs are guarded and farmlands are garrisoned around a city of evil.

In Book 1: **AVENGING ANGEL,** Jake Strait is caught in a maze of political deceit that will drench the city in a shower of spilled blood.